SADDLEBAG DISPATCHES MAGAZINE PRESENTS

GREED, GOLD, AND GUNSMOKE

STRIKE IT RICH OR DIE TRYING

Saddlebag Dispatches, LCC
A Subsidiary of Oghma Communications
Bentonville, Arkansas
www.saddlebagdispatches.com

Greed, Gold, and Gunsmoke: Strike it Rich or Die Trying
Description: First Edition | Bentonville: Saddlebag Dispatches, 2024
Identifiers: ISBN: 979-8-89299-017-2 (trade paperback)| ISBN: 979-8-89299-018-9 (eBook)
FICTION/Westerns | FICTION/Action & Adventure |
FICTION/Thrillers/Historical

Trade Paperback edition December, 2024

Cover Design and Interior Design by Casey W. Cowan
Front Cover: *California Miner with Pack Horse* by Henry Raschen (1856-1937)
Back Cover: *Sierra Nevada* by Albert Bierstadt (1830-1902)
Editing by Anthony Wood, Dennis Doty & Don Money

SADDLEBAG DISPATCHES MAGAZINE PRESENTS

GREED, GOLD, AND

GUNSMOKE

STRIKE IT RICH OR DIE TRYING

(SD)

Indians on the Green River by Alfred Jacob Miller

TABLE OF CONTENTS

The Defiance by Frederic Remington

LIST OF ILLUSTRATIONS

Pay Dirt by Charles Marion Russell

PREFACE

GOLD. The very sound of the word stirs both the most saintly of souls and the greediest of hearts. Its glitter, its shine, and the promise of wealth have lured countless dreamers to the California gold fields, transforming some into millionaires and others into paupers. Along the treacherous trek to those golden plains, few realized how the struggle, hard work, and thirst for fortune could turn them into savages—desperate to fill their coffers with riches they might never live to enjoy. Gold is the stuff of joy and ruin, rarely anything in between.

Welcome to *Greed, Gold, and Gunsmoke*, a heavy sack of stories brimming with tales from the California Gold Rush.

Follow the trail of a meteorologist who deserted his partner in a howling snowstorm, only to succumb to the elements himself while his partner survived. Witness the hunt for stolen gold hidden on a dude ranch, as opportunists lie in wait for the perfect moment to strike. Watch the hilarity unfold as two bumbling brothers attempt to rob the Jackdaw Bank, only to be heckled by customers who mistake the heist for an elaborate stage play. Hear the true confessions of Joaquin Murrieta, the legendary Robin Hood of the West, as he attempts to salvage his reputation over a deck of cards and a half-empty bottle of rotgut whiskey.

Experience the heartbreak of a man in love as he faces the possibility of losing both his girl and his place on the ranch to a "half-breed" Indian. Listen to the sweet fiddle tunes of an old man who brought the Lord's presence to a lawless town, giving it a name and a newfound purpose. And follow the journal of a fortune-seeker whose writings changed the rush for gold into a hunt for silver.

Gold Rush. The very words stir the heart and inflame the soul with dreams of glittering riches that can ruin a good life or make a bad one better. So belly up to the bar, order a bottle of rye whiskey, and enjoy these captivating tales of men and women brought to life by authors Lynn Downey, Big Jim Williams, Barbara Clouse, Tony Masero, and others who spin vivid stories of fortune hunters seeking their destinies in the California Gold Rush—and beyond.

—Anthony Wood
Managing Editor, *Saddlebag Dispatches*
November 26, 2024

SADDLEBAG DISPATCHES MAGAZINE PRESENTS

GREED, GOLD, AND GUNSMOKE

STRIKE IT RICH OR DIE TRYING

Whose Meat? by Charles Marion Russell

LEGEND OF A FORTY-NINER

TONY MASERO

YOU SEE THAT arroyo down there, the one past the big Saguaro? Well, that's where they think they killed me. They will never do that, and I am here to tell you so.

But it is a hot day and maybe you don't want to hear this story? I am looking at you and you at me, well you have paid your dollar so, bueno, I will tell you, what else is there to do here in this heat but kill flies and drink beer?

I am a handsome man in his twenty-fourth year, as you will see by my face, but my story starts when I was younger. In those days before the events that brought me here, I was a simple man, newlywed and eager for life. I lived on my family land and was content, though times were hard it is true to say, and it was this discontent that put in my mind the will to move on.

It was the year of 1850, when it was decided, and we left our home. The family had a big discussion beforehand. That is how it is always done with my people. Everybody has to have his say—brothers, cousins, uncles, you name it. Many spoke and laid out their

opinions. The old people were slow to accept the notion, but gradually they came around. Why not take the chance? It was possible
that there was plenty to be made, and success could change all our
lives for the better.

So it was agreed, and I left Sonora with my little brother and
my wife, and we traveled to California. The war with Mexico was
over two years ago, and the Americans owned that country now. It
would be difficult to survive, we knew that, but we were young and
were ready to work hard. The big news was all about the gold to be
found in those California fields, and we knew how to dig—oh, yes,
we could dig, believe me. Had we not done so often enough on our
own lands?

We arrived to a world of utter madness. To see how many came
there, so many, more people than pebbles in a riverbed. All of them
searching for gold, working in the streams and holes in the ground,
so many they covered the place as swarming ants on a hill when their
nest is disturbed. They flooded the land until it seethed. There were
no roads to speak of and nowhere to live. Towns were made of anything found. All were rough huts and tents, even the deserted ships
in San Francisco harbor were broken up and used as housing. Their
filth abounded with the vilest of people present. Gambling came
there, drinking and women of ill repute, nothing was sacred even the
old mission houses were overtaken and defiled. It was a wild country
with no order, so that the military were at a loss as they could not
control affairs with so many of their soldiers running off to seek a
fortune in the mines.

So, we found a place to stake a claim in the Sierra Nevada gold field
and were not made welcome from the very beginning. The Americans resented us and at every opportunity would revile us. They said
we had lost the war and were not welcome in what was now their

land. Even though there were many from other places, whites from Europe, dusky folk from the Sandwich Islands, and even people from China, all of them foreigners, and yet still, we were the outsiders even though our people had lived there for many hundreds of years.

So we labored and made the best of things as we could.

In time, a great crime was committed against my family, and in that, my little brother was accused of theft. They said he stole a mule, but anyone will tell you that he came here with that mule, it carried our supplies all the way from Mexico. The Americans would not listen though. They took him by force and hung him by the neck from a tree. Me, as I objected and pled his case, they only tied to a post and beat with a whip, but my poor little brother died on that rope. It was our claim that they wanted, and so, they committed the terrible act, but a worse one was to follow when, in continuing horror, they took my young wife and abused her one after the other unto death.

This I could not accept and would not take easily, and hate began to grow in my heart as a thorny Mesquite will grow in the sand, for I was not a violent man until that moment. Such rage burned in my heart and such a cry for vengeance against those that had so afflicted us that I roared at the sky and God so great was my animosity. It was in such wildness that I took my first steps along a road that only promised sin and infamy in the sight of men and the Lord.

The first I killed was a dealer in horses, a tall man and proud, so proud he could not believe it when I used my knife on his throat. That gave me a horse to ride and many other horses of his, also a rifle and a pistol that the man carried at his side. From then it was easy to exact my revenge. I could strike wherever I wanted, and so I did. Soon many others so disposed were gathering around me, and we banded together and raided the farms and dwellings, to kill and burn. The indigenous Indians were also being driven from their land and became good companions during our plunder for they had cunning and skill and knew the land.

Our name went before us and with it went fear.

We were the *banditti*.

Many unsuspecting people left the diggings with gold in their saddlebags, and for these we waited in ambush and took from them what we did not have to dig out for ourselves. No one was safe from our predation. We stole from Chinamen miners and even killed a soldier general one time. But there was even greater pleasure when those that had slain my wife and brother met their fate at my hand. To those I gave no mercy, despite their pleas, and their blood is a red stain marking the yellow gold and greed of California.

Then came a man once a soldier and deputy sheriff, a longhaired bearded man. He was brawny of body but with sly eyes and a cross-draw revolver in his belt. A brutish American and they called him a Californian Ranger with special dispensation from the governor to hunt us down. With him came others of like mind, and they scoured the countryside to find us all, eager as they were for the one thousand dollar reward.

So they hounded the land, riding this way and that until it became wise for us to leave the gold fields and make our way to a new country.

But wait—here he comes, and I will be still for now and allow him his moment.

———————⋘⋙———————

HOWDY THERE, FOLKS, *good day to all. Yes, indeed, I am the same Ranger that brought this wretch to task. Now, you will have heard the stories, the tales and legends about him, but I am here to tell you it ain't true, not one word of it. No, he weren't nothing but a lyin' murdering lowdown scoundrel who deserved all he got. Them songs you've heard about what a fine young upstanding brigand he was with a giving tendency and charity to all, that ain't nothing but bullshit of the finest kind, if you'll pardon my language. This here fellow was a party to heinous murder and calumnies of the lowest variety.*

You've seen a snake with its head cut off, ain't you, ma'am? No, well how about you, sir? You seen how it don't die right off, it writhes and rolls, now don't it? Curls itself about itself like knotted rope. Well, that's like our fella here, he just goes on even though we done cut off his sorry head just like that there snake.

Now, as you well may know, I come along at the governor's special request, and I knowed a few old boys from back in the day. They served along of me, and they was bold young men right quick of wit and sharp of eye. They cut a fine jig, I can tell you. Well, me and them and a few others, there was twenty of us all told, we took after them rascals, and one day we come across one of his kin. So we took this fellow into custody, and not to put too fine a point on it, we held him to account. You will spill the beans, old boy, we said, or we will spill your constitution all over this here dirt and then bury you under it.

What? What's that you say? Sure he did. Didn't have no choice, did he? We had him under threat of judicial punishment, that's a given, and he knowed it. Did he sing? Lord bless my soul, if he didn't ring out like a chapel bell on holy Sunday.

Well, I know y'all come here for a show of sorts, and you all paid your due, but here's the way of it. I am here to tell you, no villain in this great land can escape the proper wrath of the law, at least not under my watch that is. So y'all take your time and have your pleasure in enjoyment at this exposition but don't go pushing and pulling. Keep that line coming and I'll see you at the other end to shake your hand and bid you a good farewell.

SO, THE RANGER takes his leave and goes walking away. He was a veritable foe some of you might say, but I don't say it. No, it was only by deception that it ended with this imprisonment.

We were betrayed by one of our own, my own brother-in-law, who led them to our hidden camp where we had many horses that we had taken. There was a battle fought there, a great fight with many lost in my band. We were brave, my men and I. We fought with bullets flying all around, but we were overwhelmed. And this man, this lawman said he killed me dead and took my head as proof of his victory. He pickled this head that was laid in a great glass jar of brandy for preservation and then carried it around the whole country to be seen by people such as yourselves.

But even then, I am here to tell you that such is my position now that I can see what waits ahead for such a man. With the reward in his hand, misfortune follows this Ranger. The home he has made for himself with the money is lost to him by storm and drought and debt. He marries a wealthy woman, yet she comes to hate him and his troublesome ways. A large woman, it is said, but strong and shrewd and equipped with a sharp tongue, but even so, she is ill served by one so brutal as this Ranger made rotten by his days. This lady takes to herself a guardian in defense against his advances, yet he would not have it so and lies in wait to bring a challenge to the guard. They fight with pistols, and the Ranger is sore wounded in the shoulder so bad that his arm has to be cut off from his body. And so he dies under that knife, were it that justice had been better served and his head that was taken off instead of his arm. Yet still he dies and that fortune he made from the reward does him little good in the end.

So there you have the story, you onlookers, who stare at me dimly through the liquid in this glass. You have paid your fee for the pleasure and would think this story ends here but it does not. I live and will be remembered in song and verse as one who served his name with pride and honor and made war against those that would bring him harm. A thief? Yes, some say that, and others tell that it is someone else inside this bottle, some poor stranger taken in excuse and used as means of reward. Maybe it is true, and maybe it is not, that only you may decide.

My name, if you will ask my friends, I am called Joaquín Murrieta Carrillo of Hermosillo in Sonora.

———————

—Tony Masero, born in the UK now living in Portugal. Early career as an illustrator, including cover work for many Western series including top selling Edge and Steele books. More references can be found on his Facebook page. Since 2010 writing Western and Thrillers with published books in print and digital editions with; Black Horse (Robert Hale Books), Solstice Publishing Inc., Piccadilly Publishing, Edition Bareklau & Der Roman-Kiosk (Germany), Bold Venture Press, Pale Horse Publications, Dusty Saddle Publishing, and Wolfpack Publishing.

Trouble on the Pony Express by Frank Tenney Johnson

THE SECRET PEOPLE

TERRY CAMPBELL

I PRESSED MY back into the rear wall of the Hangman's Tree Saloon, sweating like a frustrated hog wallowing in a dry mud hole and gasping for air. I tried as hard as I could to melt into the rough pine slats. I don't know how far I'd managed to run, but I figured it had been just about a non-stop sprint from the foothills of the Sierra Nevadas into downtown Placerville. I could still hear the shouts of my pursuers around the corner. I was praying they would grow more distant, that they would tire of the chase and wander off, but as my luck would have it, they were only getting closer and more determined to find me. I tried to control my labored breaths, for I was sure they would hear me wheezing in the shadows. Clutched in my clammy hands was the reason I was in this peck of trouble in the first place—a small buckskin bag stuffed full of gold flakes. I had stolen it only a few hours earlier, a feat which culminated in my being chased down like a rabbit by a starving coyote. That would ultimately lead me into the land of the Secret People.

I tensed and tried to hold my breath when I heard the voices of two men at the entrance to the alley that ran behind the saloon. There was a reason this town was sometimes referred to as Hangtown, and if this gang of curly wolves caught me, it was likely I would experience that displeasure firsthand.

I tried to talk myself out of this foolhardy undertaking, but I rarely listen to the rational side of myself. I had been observing this small group of forty-niners panning for gold in the foothills, and I knew they were finding enough to make things tempting for me. I waited around until they stopped to go hunting for their supper, leaving one lone man in camp to begin their meal preparations. It wasn't much of a challenge to trick him into walking away while I snatched a bag of their rewards. Everything would've gone off without a hitch, but as usual, my timing was unbelievably bad. The others returned with a small cleaned and dressed doe just as I was creeping away, and the chase was on.

I recognized one of the men. Ace Winters. He and I had been on several cattle drives from Texas to Dodge City, and if I knew him, it was a safe bet Ace had recognized me as well. That meant they knew who I was. If they didn't get me, they would soon have Sheriff Rogers after me as well.

The voices at the end of the alley sounded further away, and I was relieved to discover that the two had moved on down the street. My breath was slowly returning to normal. I released a sigh of relief.

That's when the dog started barking.

You know I love dogs, but if I wasn't toting empty chambers in my Colt, I would've dropped that damned dog right there in the alley. Surely all the ruckus would bring the miners straight to me.

"Buster, are you chasing that ol' alley cat again?"

The boy was about ten years old, and he noticed me right after he made the cat query. He was munching on an apple. "Kid, shut that dog up," I whispered through clenched teeth.

The kid stared me up and down. "He ain't my dog. He's just a stray that follows me around sometimes."

"Well, shut him up, will ya?"

"Who you running from, mister?" he asked.

The kid's presence seemed to calm Buster, and he stopped barking. "Ain't running from nobody." I eyeballed the kid in return. He was grungy and disheveled. "Where'd you get that apple?"

He pointed beyond the saloon walls. "Nipped it from in front of the hardware store." He took a big crunchy bite, and milky juice dribbled down his chin. It looked mighty tasty to a man who had just run a hundred miles dodging bullets.

"You got another one?" I asked.

He eyed me suspiciously for a moment, then dug into his coat pocket and retrieved a big reddish-green apple and tossed it to me. "My name's Tommy. What's yours?"

I bit into the apple. It was the best tasting damn apple I'd ever had, I swear. "Cecil," I said through the mouthful.

"Why were those men chasing you? Did you nip apples from them?"

I chuckled. "Something bigger than apples, I'm afraid. Say, this hardware store, do they sell bullets?"

If I was going to head back up into those foothills and try to jump that claim, I was going to need lots of bullets. And if I know my fool self like I know I do, that's exactly what I was going to do.

Tommy said that he was sure it did. Placerville Hardware Store was the name of it. "You reckon they'll take gold dust as payment?"

Tommy shrugged. I cocked my head and listened. There were no shouts from my friends, and I figured it safe to exit the safety of the alley.

"Show me where the store is, kid?"

"If you'll buy me some apples," he said.

"Sure, kid. Sure. Apples it is."

THE AFTERNOON SUN was slowly beginning to dip a little lower in the sky by the time I walked out of Placerville Hardware. My coat pockets were heavy with the extra bullets I'd purchased, and my Colt was now fully loaded and ready for what may come.

Tommy was still following me around. Sometimes, Buster tagged along after us. Other times, he wandered off sniffing the ground. Sometimes, he licked his balls.

"Mister Cecil, are you going back up there? To swipe more gold from those men?"

A calmer head had prevailed since my near-death experience, and by then, I had come up with a better plan. "I'm going back up there, but I don't plan to do no more thieving. I'm going to try to come by it honest."

"How do you figure that?"

"Well, those forty-niners were finding a good deal of gold dust in those mountain streams. I figure, if I circumnavigate their claim, I might be able to locate the source. You know, beat 'em to the punch."

"Circum—what's that?" Tommy asked.

"Circumnavigate," I said. "It means, to go around, to bypass a particular area."

"Why didn't you just say that?"

I laughed. I liked this kid. He told it like it is, and he had a smart mouth and a cocky way about him. He reminded me a lot of myself at that age. It saddened me to think that he was likely surviving on the streets of Placerville with little or no parenting.

Tommy looked up at me as we continued past the storefronts. "So, you're going farther up into the mountains? Aren't you scared of the Secret People?"

It was my turn to look at him. "Secret People?"

He nodded.

"Do you mean Indians?"

Tommy shook his head. "I don't think they're Indians. It was the Indians that told us about them."

"Then who are the Secret People?"

"No one knows. But everyone knows they're there. Way up high in the mountains. Some people say they're giants."

"Oh, come on," I guffawed. "Ain't no such thing as giants."

"Well, that's what they say, is all," Tommy said. He sounded like he was getting flustered at me, and that was as good a time as any for us to part ways. I had rented a mule to carry me up into the mountains.

"Well, boy, this is where we say goodbye," I told him. "I'm going to pick up my mule and load him up, and then I'm headed out."

"I want to go with you," he protested.

"Oh, no," I said. "Those mountains are no place for a boy your age. Anyways, there's no telling what kind of trouble I might run into. I don't want to be responsible for you."

"I can take care of myself," he said.

"And I'm sure you can to some degree. But it's not going to be here, and it's not going to be with me."

I left him standing there in front of the candy store in Placerville clutching a few pennies I'd given him to lure him inside and away from me. I could feel his eyes boring into me as I walked away, but I never looked back.

THE TREES WERE throwing long shadows across the stream by the time I made it back up to the same area where I had helped myself to the hard-earned loot of Ace Winters and his merry band of gold chasers. I was sure I was close to where they'd been earlier, but it seemed they'd moved their camp. And if I hadn't passed it coming up, that only meant that they were going upward as well.

I stopped and stood as still as possible, listening for any signs of the campers. And that's when it hit me. My surroundings were silent save for my mule swishing her tail at flies. It was eerily silent. *Too silent.*

The birds had stopped chirping. Sure, they would all be roosting soon, but for all activity to suddenly cease wasn't right. It seemed even the *wind* had stopped.

Why, oh why, did I choose that moment for the Secret People to pop up in my thoughts? Getting distracted by that notion was almost a fatal mistake.

I heard the click of the hammer a second before I felt the cold steel barrel press into the back of my skull.

"Well, well, well, Cecil," a voice said. "I thought that was you I saw earlier. You back to try to rob us some more, are you?"

It was Ace, and he had me dead to rights. "Ace, old buddy. What a surprise running into you out here."

"Turn around real slow like, cowhand," he said. "Don't try your luck with me."

I did as I was told. What else could I do?

He hollered up the hillside to the others. I heard a few shouts in return, but by this time, I wasn't paying any attention to what was said. I was busy looking straight down the barrel at my destiny.

Ace kept his revolver straight and true, now aimed directly between my eyes. "How've you been, Cec? Still running the trails, or did that not work out for you?" He was right in my face.

"I see mining's no better for your polecat breath than cattle driving was," I said. Sometimes, my mouth does things before my brain can stop it. The smile on Ace's face turned to a frown, and his grip tightened on his weapon. I closed my eyes.

That's when Ace howled in pain and let his weapon fly, grabbing at his now empty gun hand and dancing around, first one foot, then the other. When he bounced back toward me, I swung my foot forward with everything I had and connected dead solid with his balls. Ace's lungs emptied in a whoosh of stinky air, and he dropped to his knees, clutching his crotch and wiggling on the ground.

I don't know what the hell happened, but I wasn't asking questions. I left my rented mule standing there by the stream, and for the second time in less than twenty-four hours, I was hightailing it back toward town, certain that we were going to have a replay of earlier events. At least I had a fully loaded gun this time.

I hadn't gone but a few hundred yards down the hill when the screaming commenced.

I stopped suddenly and wheeled about. All sorts of hell had broken out back up the mountain. I could hear gunfire and shouts and the most god awful blood-curdling screams I'd ever witnessed. They say a panther sounds like a woman screaming, but this was worse. More high-pitched. More terrified. I could hear thumps and whacks and wet scrunching sounds.

And something else, some kind of shrieking roar that made the hair on the back of my neck stick straight out.

It couldn't have been more than ten minutes, and that same peculiar dead silence filled the evening air. On top of that, it was starting to get chilly.

I say this a lot. Against my better judgment, I started to climb back up the hillside to where I'd heard all the commotion. Curiosity was part of the reason, yes, but the lure of easy pickings for already-mined gold dust was just too powerful.

My steps grew heavier and more cautious. I could see splashes of color through the trees on the ground up ahead. The blue of denim, the beige of canvas tents.

And red. Lots and lots of red. *Blood.*

And the biggest blamed footprints I'd even seen in my life.

I stopped where Ace had found me, and I just stood there, silent and unbelieving, for what felt like hours.

The gold diggers had been slaughtered. Torn to pieces. Ace's head sat resting on a boulder next to the water. His body was half-submerged in the stream, caught in a bramble. I recognized his shirt.

I worked a few evenings at a slaughterhouse outside of Fort Worth, Texas between cattle drives a few years back. I saw more blood in that place than a man could ever care to see.

What I was staring at now made that slaughterhouse look like a paint factory floor.

I bent over and emptied the contents of my guts.

Over the noise of my retching, I heard something behind me. I spun quickly about and fumbled for my Colt. If it had been real trouble, I once again would've been dead. My hands were shaking that much.

But it wasn't trouble.

It was Tommy. The little shit had followed me after all.

"T-Tommy," I began, my words barely squeaking from my lips. "What the hell are you doing here?"

"I wanted to go with you," he said.

It was then that I noticed the slingshot clutched in his little hands. That's when I knew. Hard to stay mad at a kid when there's a good chance he'd saved your sorry neck.

I reached out and ruffled the hair on his head.

"You steal more gold?" he asked.

It was then that I figured I should be shielding him from the gruesome carnage all around him. I've never been no 'count with kids. I don't know what to do with them.

Instead, we both stood there, dumbstruck.

Finally, I looked down at him. "The Secret People."

He slowly nodded his head. "I told you."

I don't begin to understand what had happened only moments earlier. I gathered my mule and borrowed another from the dead miners for Tommy and helped myself to a few more pouches of their bounty. They weren't going to need it.

"Let's go, Tommy. I expect we should report this to the sheriff. He'll have to see it for himself. 'Cause I suspect he ain't gonna believe it otherwise."

THE LOCAL AUTHORITIES chalked up the deaths of the seven panners in the Sierra Nevada Mountains to grizzly bears. Sounded good to me. No one explained the footprints, though. Just kind of ignored them.

I stayed in the same area for another six weeks or so. Yes, against my better judgment. I never saw the Secret People, but I could hear them whooping way back in the distance, knocking on trees, sometimes moving through the underbrush. If they thought I'd gotten too close, I'd get a large stone lobbed at me as a warning.

I never struck it rich like I always did in my dreams, but I did coax enough gold out of that stream to get my fool self back home to Texas. I bought some land near Alpine, a dozen head of longhorns, and started my own cattle ranch. I'm living the good life now.

Turns out Tommy didn't have any family in Placerville. Indians had killed his parents, and he'd run away from the orphanage they'd placed him in. So, the only Christian thing I could do was bring him along. Once we got settled in Texas, I officially adopted him. He helps me out on the ranch a lot, but he still has a smart mouth.

I think about the Secret People from time to time. Part of me is angry that I never got to see them, but the rest of me is thankful for that, because it probably wouldn't have ended well for me.

I've heard stories about them since. The Indians called them sasquatch. More and more encounters were reported with the steady influx of gold-seekers. Some people came up missing, some were found killed by "wild animals."

There are things out there in this world that man knows very little about. Even here in Alpine, cattle come up missing. Some are found dead and drained of blood. Chupacabras, some of the Mexicans I've hired as ranch hands say. Whatever that is.

Tommy and I often sit on the front porch in the evenings and discuss the Secret People. He has his theories, I have mine.

I said goodbye to my thieving days long ago. Tommy too. The only things we nibble these days are apples.

Apples that we bought fair and square.

From money we made from the gold we took out of the land of the Secret People.

Or, more likely, that we were *allowed* to take.

———————❦———————

—Terry Campbell is a soon-to-be-60-year-old writer/artist living in McKinney, Texas with his lovely wife and two hairless dogs. He is currently hard at work creating fiction and converting his art studio into an awesome writing den/library. Terry self-published his first novel, Kindred Feather, *in 2023.*

ELEANOR DUMONT AND THE FRISCO GAME

TERRY ALEXANDER

"MISS DUMONT, COULD I interest you in a few hands of poker?" The man wore a tailored suit and spoke in a cultured manner. He removed a handkerchief from his suit and mopped his brow. "You seem to have driven all your players away."

"Thank you for your kind offer, Mister Stuart. It has been a long day, and I'm very tired. I believe I'll retire to my room and rest for the remainder of the evening." Eleanor bowed her head.

"Please call me Silas. Surely, you won't reject the opportunity to spend some time with a fellow southerner. There are so few of us in California." A broad grin split Stuart's face. "Just a few hands before we call it a night."

"It would be something to tell everyone if you would sit in for a few hands." A chubby man with a spotted tie looked up at the pretty woman and grinned. "It's not often I have a beautiful woman at my table."

Eleanor grinned. She brushed at the thin line of hair above her upper lip and nodded. "Okay, Tony. I'll sit in and play a few hands. What are the stakes?"

The chubby man nodded. "The ante is twenty dollars each, and the smallest bet you can make is twenty dollars, with no upper limit."

"Here's two hundred." She pulled a stack of bills from her small purse. "Give me some chips."

"Allow me." Stuart took the bills and gave Eleanor a stack of chips in return. "We're playing five card draw with jacks or better to open. Not that French card game you fancy." He stuffed the bills in his coat pocket. "Mister McGuire will deal us each five cards, and the object is to make the best hand you can and have better cards than the other people involved in the game."

"I have played draw poker at times. Even though I don't like the game. I'm very familiar with the rules." She tossed a twenty-dollar chip to the center of the table. "Ante up."

Stuart and McGuire followed suit. McGuire tugged on his necktie and shuffled the cards. He then placed them before Stuart. "Cut." The southerner cut the deck in the center and nodded to McGuire.

"Jamie, bring me a glass of brandy from the bar," Stuart ordered.

A Black man rose from a small stool by the door and approached the bar. He licked his lips while he waited on the bartender to fill an empty glass with brandy. The bartender watched him closely as he lifted the glass from the countertop and hurried across the room. He placed the glass near Stuart's free hand.

"Here you is, Mister Stuart," he mumbled and returned to his stool by the door.

"Who is that?" Eleanor asked. "Your personal servant."

"In a manner of speaking." Stuart smiled. "My father gave him to me five years ago. I own him. He's my slave."

Eleanor shook her head. "California's not a slave state."

"It's not a state at all. It's just a territory." McGuire dealt out the cards. His eyes came up from the table and met Eleanor's. "For the time being, slavery is tolerated. If a slave escapes, however, the authorities will not pursue him. There are no slave catchers here."

"I assure you. Jamie won't try to escape from me. His wife and family are back home on my family estate. If he decided to flee, his family would suffer the consequences."

Eleanor glanced toward the door. Jamie kept his head bowed. Eyes focused on the floor. "I've never cared for slavery." She lifted her cards from the table and stared at the pasteboards. "Open goes to you, Mister Stuart."

He lifted his glass to his lips and sipped the brandy. "Indeed." His fingers plucked two twenty-dollar chips from his stack and tossed them to the center of the table. "Open for forty."

"You must have a good hand." McGuire fanned out his cards. "I think I'll call. I want to see your cards."

"Are you trying to impress me, Mister Stuart?" Eleanor lifted two chips and tossed them to the center of the table. "There is your forty and forty more." She followed that with two additional chips. "I'm not easily impressed."

"I can see that." Stuart nodded. He took a sip of his brandy and tossed out three chips. "There is your raise and twenty more." He shifted his attention to McGuire. "That's sixty to you."

"Yes, it is." McGuire grinned. "I think I'll call." He tossed his chips to the center of the table. "How many cards do you want?"

"Two please." Stuart removed two cards from his fan and tossed them face down to the center of the table.

McGuire dealt him two cards from the deck, placing them face down near his stack of chips. "Now, Eleanor, how many cards would you like?"

"Three for me, Tony." She removed the discards and placed them near the pot.

He gave her the requested cards. "The dealer takes three, as well." He tossed the unwanted pasteboards to the center of the table and dealt himself three cards. He looked at his hand and shifted his eyes to Stuart. "The bet is yours."

"Since we only have Miss Dumont for a few hands, I believe I'll make the bet interesting." A smile played along his lips. "The bet is fifty."

Eleanor returned his smile. "I'll call your bet, Mister Stuart."

"Tell me, have you heard anything from Louisiana lately? My family isn't keeping me updated on the happenings back home." He glanced over to McGuire. "The bet is to you."

"I'll call." He looked from Eleanor to Silas Stuart as he tossed his chips to the center of the table."

"You have me at a disadvantage, Mister Stuart. You act as if you know me, but to my knowledge we've never met." She cocked her head to the side, her tongue protruded past her lips a fraction of an inch.

"We have met in the past, While I may not be a memorable character, you, on the other hand, are *quite* memorable." He bowed his head and laid his cards on the tabletop. "I have three tens."

Eleanor touched the fine line of hair above her top lip. She had heard the vulgar nickname that some men applied to her. Calling her "Madame Mustache" behind her back. "I have three Queens."

"The pot is yours, Eleanor." McGuire tossed his cards to the center of the table.

Eleanor raked her winnings toward her. "I believe the deal is yours, Mister Stuart."

"Yes, it is." Stuart drained the brandy and turned his head toward Jamie. "Fetch me another glass." He held the empty glass above his head. "Would you two care for anything? Jamie would be happy to fetch it for you."

"No, I'm fine. Thank you." Eleanor arranged her chips in a stack and tossed a twenty-dollar chip to the center. She met Jamie's eyes when the man approached the table. The slave took the glass from Stuart's hand and walked to the bar. He returned within seconds with a filled glass. He placed the glass on the table and departed back to his stool without saying a word.

"Here are the cards, Silas." McGuire placed the cards in front of the southerner.

He lifted the deck and nodded. "I believe I'd like to raise the limit on this hand, say the low bet is fifty dollars."

"That's very irregular. Neither I nor Miss Dumont are prepared for such a game." McGuire thumped the table with his index finger. "A change in the rules should be discussed early in the evening, not at the last few minutes of the evening."

"But that's precisely why I'd like to do it. I won't have another opportunity to play against Miss Dumont. She'll be running her own game tomorrow." Stuart shuffled the cards. "I want to be able to tell everyone that I played poker against the best woman player in all of California."

"I'll play until I run out of chips. Then I'm going to retire for the evening." Eleanor nodded.

"Wonderful." Stuart placed the cards before her. "Cut."

She reached forward and tapped the top card. "Deal."

Stuart lifted the deck and began to deal the cards. He had a habit of humming as he dealt. He finished the deal and looked at his hand. "If I wasn't the dealer, I'd swear the man gave me a terrible hand on purpose." He glanced at Eleanor. "What say you, can you open?"

Eleanor lifted her cards. She had a pair of Jacks. She nodded and tossed three chips to the center of the table. "Bet sixty."

"I'm out." McGuire shook his head. "No point in playing this hand."

"The pot is yours again, Miss Dumont. I yield the deck to your skillful hands." He threw his cards to the center and placed the deck near Eleanor's hands.

"This isn't much of a pot." She raked the money toward her.

The sound of running boots echoed from the boardwalk. A tall man with a bloody head, torn shirt, and a whip marked back ran inside. "Help me. The vigilante committee did this to me." He crouched down near Jamie.

Stuart rose to his feet. "You need to leave, right now. The committee has marked you as a thief. They'll parade you around town as a warning to any other thieves before they hang you. He advanced toward the injured man. "Get out of here before they find you and punish us all."

"Silas is right. You must move on." McGuire drew a .30 caliber pepperbox pistol from his coat. "I don't want any problems with the vigilantes."

"Where did you come from?" Eleanor dropped the cards on the table. She pulled a cleaning cloth from a nearby table and approached the man. "Did you know anyone in the group?"

He snatched the cloth from her hand and held it to the bloody holes where his ears used to be. "My name's Doyle Williams. I was on the schooner *Ohio* until last Wednesday when I jumped ship." The blood covered the rag within seconds.

"Get away from him, Miss Dumont." Stuart stepped to the far side of the table, allowing himself a clear field of vision, but kept him behind McGuire in case the shorter man had to shoot. "You can't give this man aide. The vigilantes won't hesitate to punish you if you cross them."

"The man is a thief. The committee gave him a trial. He was punished according to a miner's court." McGuire cocked the pistol's hammer. "If he'd killed his victim, they would have cut off his lips and blinded him as well before his death. Now please step away from him."

"Tony, I'm getting out of here," the bartender mumbled. "I'm not going to be around when the vigilance committee gets here."

"Get out of here, Tom. I'll see you tomorrow." McGuire said. He turned his head as the bartender disappeared out the back door. "You can rest for a few minutes, then you have to leave."

"You're willing to stand there and see him suffer?" Eleanor turned to face the two men. "Are you going to watch the vigilantes hang him, as well?"

"We can't cross those people, not if we want to stay in this city." Stuart shook his head. "If they think that we're against them, we'll be tarred and feathered and run out of town on a rail."

"I recognize you." Williams pointed at Stuart. "You were at the docks when I jumped ship." His gaze switched to Jamie. *"Both* of you were at the docks. You helped me rob that miner. You got part of the gold."

Jamie jumped from his stool. "You get away from me. Now."

"What's he talking about, Stuart? Did you help him rob a miner?" Eleanor turned and stared at the southerner. "Are you a thief?"

"That man is talking nonsense. Do I look like a thief to you?" Stuart held his coat open, showing off his expensive clothes.

"Stay where you are. Tell your servant to stand still. I don't want to shoot anyone until I know what is going on." McGuire pointed the pistol toward Stuart then at Jamie.

Eleanor turned her attention toward Jamie. "Did you see this man down at the docks?"

Jamie cast wide eyes toward Stuart.

"He's not going to hurt you." Eleanor took a step toward him. "Tell me, did you see this man at the docks?"

"Keep your mouth shut, Jamie. Your family is still in Louisiana." Stuart glanced at the pistol in McGuire's hand. "You should point that somewhere else. When the committee arrives, they'll be displeased when I tell them how you sided with this man."

Eleanor took the pistol from McGuire's hand. "If they arrive and you open your mouth, you'll be the first man shot."

"It's foolish to protect a thief from the vigilantes." Stuart raised his hands above his head.

"Now, Jamie. Have you seen this man before?" She pointed the weapon at Doyle.

Jamie nodded. "Yes miss, I have. We saw him at the docks last week." He licked his lips and glanced over to Stuart. "Massa Stuart helped him rob a man in one of the alleys down there. They beat him over the head with a club and took his gold."

"You won't ever see your family again. I'll make sure they get sold off and shipped out of Louisiana." Stuart's arms dropped. "I'll whip the hide from your back. You'll wish that you hadn't crossed me."

McGuire turned to face Stuart. "You won't be whipping anyone. Not in my saloon."

"The man is my property. He belongs to *me*. I'll whip him if I please." Stuart glared at the shorter man.

"I'm sorry. Massa Stuart. I'm sorry. Don't take it out on my family." Tears streamed down Jamie's face. "Please, don't sell my family."

"You should have thought of that before you opened your mouth." Stuart nodded. "Before we sell them, we'll let Mister Shavers have his way with them for a little while."

"Not Mister Shavers. He loves to whip my kind." Jamie backed away. His knees bumped into his stool. The injured man grabbed his hand and pulled himself to his feet. He left a smear of crimson on Jamie's hand and clothes.

"He won't do anything to your family." Eleanor pointed the weapon at Stuart. "I'll see that he doesn't bother your family."

"That's the biggest lie told today." Stuart laughed. "What can you do to stop me? One word from me and his entire family will know nothing but torment." A grin stretched his face. "I only wish I could be there to see your grandmother being punished for your transgression."

"You won't punish my grandma. Not my grandma." Jamie yanked a knife from his jacket and raced toward Stuart. Within seconds he buried the knife to the hilt in the southerner's chest.

He dropped to his knees. His hands clutching at Jamie. "I didn't think you'd attack me like this." His hand closed on the handle, he tried to pull the blade free, but gave up after the attempt. The color drained from his face, leaving it a pasty white mask of pain. "Your family will die a painful death."

Jamie yanked the knife free and plunged it into Stuart's neck. The gambler's eyes rolled back in his head. A long "oh" came from his lips as the last bit of air rushed from his lungs. "I don't regret killing him. He was a cruel man. He enjoyed inflicting punishment on folks like me." He licked his lips. "We have to keep his death a secret. We can't let his family know he's gone. They'll punish my family for sure."

Eleanor eased the hammer down on the pistol and passed it gingerly back to McGuire. "I don't think I'll be needing this." She glanced from Jamie to Doyle. "We still need to figure out what to do with you, though. The vigilantes will be here before you know it. If they find you, they'll hang you for sure." She glanced toward McGuire. "Do you have any ideas?"

"There's a ship leaving at six in the morning. It's going down the coast to old Mexico. I know the captain, for a couple of hundred dollars he'll let them hide out in the cargo hold." McGuire rubbed the back of his neck. "If someone finds them on the ship, he won't try to help. They'll be on their own."

"I've got money on the table there." Eleanor nodded toward the table. "Stuart won't be needing his money where he's going." She shifted her gaze to Jamie. "You'll have to travel cross country for a long way to get back to Louisiana."

"I'll make it." He nodded.

"When I get healed up, I'll help him get there," Doyle said.

"Stuart had over seventeen hundred dollars on him. With the money you had on the table that's over two thousand." McGuire stuffed the money into a wallet and gave it to Jamie. "Keep this hidden. If anyone sees you carrying that kind of money your life won't be worth nothing."

"You three need to get out that back door. I hear the vigilantes coming closer." The rumble of tramping feet on the boardwalk came to their ears. "Get moving."

"What about you?" Doyle asked. "What are you going to tell the vigilantes? How are you going to explain him?"

"I'll tell them that I killed him." Eleanor nodded. "He tried to get rough with me and I stabbed him with a knife I won from a tin horn last week." She glanced at Jamie. "I'll make sure word gets to his family in Louisiana. His kin will blame me and not you, your family shouldn't be in any danger."

"Thank you." Jamie licked his lips. "I'll find a way to repay you for helping me."

"We'll find a way to repay you," Doyle said.

"We need to get going. Those footsteps are getting closer." McGuire walked toward the back door.

Eleanor watched them leave.

—*Terry Alexander and his wife, Phyllis, live on a small farm near Porum, Oklahoma. They have three children, thirteen grandchildren, and four great grandchildren. If you see him at a conference, though, don't let him convince you to take part in one of his trivia games—he'll stump you every time.*

The Last Drop by Charles Schreyvogel

JOAQUIN MURRIETA'S CONFESSIONS

STEVEN MCFANN

HE GAZES AT the lifeless eyes behind the glass. The dead man shares his name, but beyond their mutual national origin, he feels no kinship with the pickled head he paid a dollar to see.

The museum docent informs him that his time is up. A small crowd forms behind him hoping to see the head of the outlaw Joaquin Murrieta. The museum guests, all of them urbanites unaccustomed to seeing a Mexican dressed muy rural in his hat and boots, gawk at the old *vaquero* as he passes by.

He walks through San Francisco, a city whose cosmopolitan face hides its frontier soul. Some districts he doesn't recognize. Others, like Chinatown and the Barbary Coast, he knows too well.

He sits at a lunch counter in a neighborhood too wealthy and Anglo for men like him. He flips through the pages of the journal he's scribbled in for years and waits for the daughter of an old friend, the last living man who knew the truth about him. The truth he plans to provide the daughter in the pages of the journal. Pages that contain who he is and who he was.

HIS FATHER PASSED only his name to him before fleeing for reasons unknown to him and unmentioned by his mother. Her marriage to a ranchero saved them from poverty, but Don Carillo felt no fondness for the bastard who bore the same name as his wandering father, Joaquin Murrieta.

At sixteen, he lived at a Sonoran mission as a student. His stepfather told him he should feel honored to receive an expensive church education, but the youth understood he was unwanted. He avoided studies to watch the nearby *vaqueros* whose freedom he envied.

A detachment of soldiers brought American prisoners to be detained on the mission grounds. One caught his attention, a man merely seven years his senior whose sad blue eyes bore the pain of a man aged far beyond his years. When Joaquin met him, those blue eyes gazed with reverence toward a statue of the Virgin in the mission garden.

"I didn't know *Yanquis* could be Catholic," he said. Father Castillo claimed America was a Godless land.

The *Yanqui* laughed. He spoke flawless Spanish. "Sorry to disappoint you."

The *Yanqui's* name was Bill Byrnes. He was a seminary dropout who traded God for guns and found adventure in Texas. His tales of Comanche fights along the Rio Bravo wowed Joaquin. They played cards until dawn, sharing drinks stolen from the soldiers. Bill told him that wielding a gun is the closest a man comes to possessing God's power. He shared with Joaquin his desire to see California, a rumored paradise of rich soil and green pastures where *vaqueros* and vintners alike thrived in the mild coastal climes. In Bill, Joaquin received a window to a world kept from him behind the mission walls—a world far beyond his imagination of what the world could hold for a man.

So he raised no alarm when Bill and the other Americans made their escape. He resisted brutal interrogation from the soldiers who suspected him, and he escaped the captivity of his cell. He stole a soldier's horse and rode toward no destination in mind but his own freedom.

He was found sunburned and starved when the Feliz family took him in. Their eldest son, Claudio, hired him to help herd horses. Their only daughter, Rosa, admired the rugged kid who passed Bill's tales of adventure off as his own. His marriage to her at age nineteen bound him to his foster family.

Gold fever spread south from Sutter's Mill to Sonora, and Claudio's eyes turned toward California, toward hills of gold. He took his younger brothers, Reyes and Jesús, and Joaquin followed at Rosa's insistence on remaining close to family. Joaquin had no desire for gold. The California he longed for was that which Bill Byrnes described, a pastoral paradise. The love for open land and the desire for a *vaquero's* freedom burned inside him, so he took a job wrangling horses for Robert Livermore near Niles Canyon. He spent many nights sleeping on the ground while camped in the Diablo Ranges, convinced he found paradise and praying that his old American friend Bill Byrnes found his way to California.

The dream soured fast. Claudio fell in with bad men and became their leader, dragging young Reyes with him. Joaquin declined his offer to join, but life with Rosa proved unfulfilling. They blamed each other for her failure to conceive. Word of his impotence spread among the *vaqueros,* with only a cowhand named Benito Bautista being drunk and stupid enough to tease him over it after losing at cards to him.

By dawn, Benito bled out in the Alameda Creek. Joaquin fled to the only refuge he had, Claudio Feliz's gang.

They owned the Sierra roads in the summer of '51. They painted the highways red and filled their pockets with gold. Joaquin finally understood Bill's claim that guns granted men God's power. He savored the fear in men's eyes, felt joy in the knowledge that the simple twitch of a finger could erase a man's soul from the Earth. But he lacked Claudio's talent for murder, his penchant for high risk that caused a rift between the in-laws. He peeled Claudio's men away from him, including his brother Reyes, and formed a gang who avoided Claudio's bloody fate at the Salinas River that winter.

They rustled horses from *ranchos* and sold them across the state, unglamorous work that saw them sleeping under the San Joaquin stars. The initial thrill of *la vida desesperada* faded fast with posses on their tails every morning. Indians robbed them of their horses and left them for dead in the Tehachapi Mountains. All except Reyes mutineed, and his reward for loyalty was near-death from a grizzly attack. Joaquin sat beside his recovering in-law in a mountain inn and realized a fresh start was needed. He left Reyes to recover in the care of the innkeepers and left word to reunite in Los Angeles.

Los Angeles was little more than a village of sun-bleached *adobes* along the river. Her violence made mining towns seem like monasteries. But Joaquin fell in love with that hideous scar on the beautiful basin. He laid low, trained horses, gambled, and his evening excursions through the dusty calles earned him a new woman named Ana Benites. But old demons haunted him in the City of Angels. Reyes arrived and brought trouble with him. Joaquin quickly took a stolen remuda off Reyes' hands to prevent the impetuous youth from attempting to drive them to San Jose on his own.

Instead of protecting the boy, his action condemned him. When he arrived in San Jose, he learned Reyes had been hanged based on the testimony of his woman Ana Benites. That the same fate awaited him in Los Angeles.

He drowned his impulse for revenge against Ana and the Angelenos in whiskey and turned his anger toward the whole world. His new gang reveled in mercilessness as they burned their way across the Sierra Nevada, no thought of God's wrath in his frigid heart. His became the most feared name in Gold Country.

But it brought no wealth, and it brought no release. They were driven from the mountains with little in their pockets, most of it gambled away. His men abandoned him. He snuck away on a steamer, deep in the bottle and bound for revenge in Los Angeles. But he stayed on the steamer when it reached San Pedro. California brought him only tears and blood, and his taste for revenge soured. He wanted only to escape, to flee back to Mexico and reverse life to the way it was. He sailed south toward Sinaloa and wept at the sight of the Mexican coast. He led his horse through the streets of Mazatlan and rode her toward the Sierra Madre. Toward hunger, toward wandering, and toward an uncertain end.

HE WAS FORTY years old when he learned he had been dead for seventeen years.

Seventeen years since California, the lost years. Seventeen years spent wrangling and rustling horses, fighting Frenchmen at Puebla, and smuggling goods to the Comanche in the Llano. Seventeen years failing to rediscover God at the bottom of a bottle, failing to find his place in the world. Sometimes he yearned for the domestic life he rejected. Usually he yearned for youth, a return to his desperado days.

Such yearning plagued him when he learned the news of his own alleged death from some cheap book in the hands of an American in El Paso. His name was printed in bold letters. A *vaquero* caricature adorned the cover art. The book claimed he led the most notorious gang in California as a Mexican rebel in defiance of Anglo invaders. The book claimed the California Rangers led by Captain Harry Love killed him and severed his head. He felt sick when he read the name of the Ranger who identified him.

Bill Byrnes.

He read the book obsessively on his journey back to California. Some details were true, but most of it was fantasy. Three Fingered Jack? The Five Joaquins? The author claimed his cause was spurred by revenge for the ravishment and murder of his wife by Anglo miners, a crime never committed against her. His own life had been robbed from him and reshaped into that of a Robin Hood to make lawmen and booksellers rich. He arrived in San Francisco and spent dollar after dollar visiting the head they claimed was his.

At first he pitied the man who took his place, his only crime being Mexican and a suitable substitute for Joaquin. Then he envied him. He envied the gawking crowds, the *corridos,* the dime novels, all honoring the wrong man while the real Joaquin Murrieta still breathed.

"That could have been me. That *should* have been me."

His efforts at reclaiming the infamy owed to him proved fruitless. He dropped his name to barflies who bought him drinks because they considered him an entertaining clown. Lawmen laughed at his desperate confessions.

"You know how many of you we used to get in a month?"

Even Jesús Feliz, youngest brother of Claudio and Reyes, wouldn't have him. He believed Joaquin dead for so long that the shock nearly caused him to collapse. The shock turned to rage. Rage for Joaquin's abandonment of Rosa, rage for leaving Reyes to die. Rage over the crippled leg he lived with, a gift from bounty hunters who tortured him for information on his brother-in-law.

Jesús told Joaquin, "I wish you had been dead."

Joaquin spent many days afterwards in a Monterey saloon. He became a local curiosity, the *cantina* crackpot who played monte and made claims of being the late Joaquin Murrieta. People paid him to tell stories, and he gambled it away.

During one of his storytelling sessions, he noticed a group of *vaqueros* pointing toward him from the corner. They eyed him intently. The leader approached. He introduced himself as Felipe and said he knew who the man telling tall tales truly was.

"Like I said, I'm Joaquin."

Felipe shook his head. "Oh, no. You worked up north with my oldest brother."

Felipe drew a Bowie knife. "Benito Bautista. Remember that name?"

It was a name he hadn't heard in nineteen years, but one he hadn't forgotten. The *vaquero* who insulted him. His first kill.

Joaquin knew by Felipe's eyes that he intended to kill him, and nothing except death or revenge would satisfy that intent.

He fled Monterey, chased by Felipe and his men, with no old *compadres* left in California to protect him. Joaquin knew he needed one person who would believe him. Someone to give him what he desired, a recognition of who he was and maybe, the legendary end he deserved.

There was only one man left in California who could do that.

RAINWATER DRIPPED FROM his hat as he stepped inside the El Dorado Saloon. The barkeep pointed him to the bloated man nursing a bottle in a dark corner. His sad blue eyes were bloodshot. Joaquin couldn't believe this was his old friend.

His spurs alerted Bill Byrnes to his presence. Silver streaked the Sonoran's hair and beard, but there was no mistaking Joaquin Murrieta.

Bill cackled. Joaquin pulled out a card deck.

"Play five rounds?"

"With what money?"

"If I lose, I'll pay your tab?"

"If you win?"

Joaquin dealt the cards. Bill's hands shook. He gulped whiskey to steady them.

"Guess you're a ghost."

"You know that wasn't me."

"Can't tell anymore. My mind fails me these days."

They played the agreed five rounds. Joaquin won most of them.

"So what do I owe?"

"The truth. Tell the world you killed the wrong man. That I am Joaquin Murrieta!"

"And face a murder charge?"

"You won't. Because this time, you'll get the right man."

Joaquin slid his spare revolver across the table. "Just make it clean. Let me die like a man."

Bill stood up, leaving the gun and taking the whiskey.

"You ungrateful son-of-a-bitch."

Joaquin chased him in the rain and down the muddy Placerville streets. Bill faced him, seventeen years of guilt unleashed.

"You know, I killed a lot of men, but you're the only one who haunts me. And I didn't even kill you."

"You lied for money."

"For mercy. There was no chance in hell we'd get you, and I didn't want to, but Captain Love and the other Rangers would have hunted every Mexican in this state until they found you. I didn't need an ocean of blood on my hands. I put a stop to that."

"That makes you a good man?"

"Have you looked in the mirror lately? You didn't exactly stay an altar boy."

"Then punish me. Atone for your crimes. I'll pay for mine, just let me have my name back."

"If you wanna die, why don't you get some other fool to handle it?"

"Because they don't know me," Joaquin said. "I've lived as a nobody. I don't want to die as one."

"Why not? I wish I was a nobody. Embrace it, enjoy it. I gave you almost twenty goddamn years to build a new life."

"What life? I have nothing, I have *nobody!*"

"Well, that makes two of us."

Joaquin shook his head at the pathetic figure, seeing his lowest moments in the last two decades reflected back at him.

"I used to worship you."

Bill spat. "Sorry to disappoint."

Joaquin turned his back down the street. "Forget it. You pathetic drunk, you probably can't even shoot anymore."

The gunshot made him jump. His hat flew from his head. Another two shots bounced it high in the air before it fell down to the mud. Distant voices cursed about gunfire late in the evening.

Bill holstered his smoking revolver. "It's the only thing I was ever good at."

"Why don't you ride with me?" Joaquin said. If Bill wouldn't help him meet his end, he still had to face Felipe's gang and he preferred not to do it alone.

"You dropped your hat," Bill said. He stumbled through the mud and disappeared in the darkness, fading like a memory.

HE LEFT THE hotel and wandered deep into the Sierra. He recognized old haunts. He held the soil where Claudio spilled the blood of a teamster for the hell of it. Most of the old mining camps were abandoned for company-owned hydraulic mines. Even the forest felt changed in those years.

He sensed he was being tracked. He left the road and followed the American River, finding a rocky section of the south fork to water his horse. He sat by the river, watching the water flow over the rocks.

He looked up and saw two men watching him. He heard a revolver cock behind him and saw the reflection of Felipe in the water.

"Benito died by a river, didn't he?" Felipe said. "Seems fitting, no?"

"You certainly know how to find a man," Joaquin said. One other gunman stood on his side of the river. "Can I stand?"

"You can kneel."

He dug his knees into the mud. Any sudden move to grab his guns would end it.

"Any final pleas of mercy?" Felipe asked.

"Just a statement."

Felipe nodded. Joaquin noticed a man clutching a rifle and crouched near the trees across the river. A face he thought he'd not see again.

"I am Joaquin Murrieta—"

The men laughed.

"—and your brother was a lousy card player."

Felipe snorted. "Fine. *Adios,* 'Joaquin.'"

The rifle cracked and Felipe collapsed, leaving a crimson mist where he stood. The gunman beside Joaquin pointed his gun at the trees and fired. Joaquin drew his revolver and brought the man down.

Joaquin found meager cover behind the bodies as the two gunmen turned toward the source of the shots. Joaquin knew the gunman had hit his target. All he could do was buy Bill the little time he had. He leveled his revolver on Felipe's corpse and fired. He hit one of them in the shoulder. Their attention turned toward the river and they dove for cover behind large rocks.

A bullet flew past his ear. He emptied one gun and drew his back-up revolver from his boot. He reached for Felipe's revolver, cocked it, and charged across the river.

The injured gunman fell first. Joaquin missed the last man and took cover behind a Ponderosa. He heard the crunching of feet against rock and the jingling of spurs as the last gunman approached.

Bill Byrnes bled against the opposite tree. He peered past Joaquin and mouthed "now."

The gunman passed the tree and Joaquin aimed his revolver point blank toward the man's neck and fired.

He heard the shuffling of the injured man crawling toward his revolver. Joaquin kicked it from him and placed his spur against the man's neck, drawing blood. The gunman begged. Joaquin recognized the fear in the man's eyes, an expression he once savored. But Joaquin felt no joy and no power. Only a cold sense of duty.

"You go to hell, you bastard."

Joaquin cocked his gun. "I told you. My name is Joaquin."

He let the gun have the final word.

Joaquin inspected Bill's wound. He was shot in the shoulder, close to his heart. It wouldn't be immediately fatal, but he could see the blood quickly draining from the wound and he pressed hard against it as he tied a torn piece of serape around it.

"You were following me?"

Bill nodded. "You asked me to ride with you. You left the hotel when I went back."

Bill slipped in and out of consciousness. Joaquin put him on his horse. He wrapped Bill's hands around his waist and tied his hands to the saddle horn to prevent his collapse. Bill begged for whiskey. He shivered. Joaquin realized the shaking wasn't from the wound. Bill begged and Joaquin said, *"no tengo,"* and assured him he'd be at a doctor's soon and that he wouldn't die. It was one of many bullets Bill had taken over a lifetime of fighting. He wouldn't die. He couldn't.

The Placerville doctor removed the bullet but kept Bill in his care to prevent the wound from infecting. It was too early to tell what damage it did to him. He told Joaquin to come back in a week. His tone suggested it was for the sake of Joaquin's safety to leave before lawmen questioned the situation.

Joaquin avoided town for two weeks before returning. The doctor informed him that he couldn't treat Bill at his office and sent him to a doctor in Stockton. But the Stockton doctor had already sent Bill to a hospital in town.

"You couldn't treat him?"

The Stockton doctor raised a brow. "Not for what he's got."

Joaquin waited for hours outside the asylum before any doctor would speak to him. The screams of patients penetrated the stone walls. The doctor explained that Bill suffered psychosis. They explained that he spoke of ghosts from his past coming to haunt him. Bill kept saying he couldn't be locked away. He needed to see if Joaquin was alright. When they asked who, he said "Joaquin Murrieta. My friend. The man I killed. He's waiting for me in Hangtown. I killed him, but he's not dead."

They asked Joaquin if he knew what Bill meant. Joaquin shook his head.

"How do you know him, anyway?"

"We played cards together."

"Do you want us to tell him anything?"

Joaquin shook his head. His words would be no comfort. The doctor asked his name, and Joaquin said he was nobody.

Bill Byrnes died at the asylum within two years. Joaquin didn't attend the funeral. He imagined visiting the grave, playing Monte with the headstone, and offering libations. But he never did. Leaving Bill alone in the ground was just another of the many regrets he collected in his regrettable life.

NELLIE ABBOT SITS at the lunch counter across from Joaquin. She bears the surname of her husband, but her melancholy blue eyes are unmistakably those of her father, Bill Byrnes.

Twenty years have passed since Byrnes' death. He tells Nellie that he was old friends with her father. He tells her how he brought her father to safety before he was committed, that they had been gambling friends. She seems politely skeptical.

"Where did you say you met?"

"In Mexico. During the war."

A faint sound escapes her lips. A forced smile barely masks years of buried pain.

"I suppose you also knew Murrieta, then."

He cradles the journal in his lap. "By name. Did your father speak of him?"

"Only when he was drunk. Which was often."

She says he spoke of Joaquin with more fondness than one usually speaks of someone they condemned to death. Joaquin listens, wondering whether to reveal the truth to a woman clinging to the few fond memories of an estranged father.

He tucks the journal away and tells her that Bill saved his life twice.

"I'd have preferred he saved his own life," she says. "He acted as if he didn't deserve to be happy."

They exchange no further words. He sees no need to offer the journal. There seems to be a mutual understanding between the two. An agreed upon truth that for the sake of the stranger's privacy and the sake of what little remains of her father's faded reputation, must remain unspoken.

On his way out of San Francisco, he passes a vaudeville performance of "The Life of Joaquin Murrieta, the Robin Hood of El Dorado." In the back of the crowd, a man tells two women he knew Joaquin in Los Angeles. Another man says he rode with Joaquin as his gang's cook. A painted woman says she slept with Joaquin. The man asks, "Which outlaw hasn't poked you?" and laughs.

Joaquin smirks. He laughs at the terrible mock-Mexican accent of the Anglo actor caked in bronze makeup. He laughs at the bellicose Harry Love, a man Joaquin knew only by name and reputation. He laughs at the gag of his severed head singing *corridos* to the crowd.

The following dawn, he builds a fire in Niles Canyon near the creek where he killed his first man. He sets the journal over the fire while roasting coffee. He watches the pages shrivel under the flames and sips coffee and imagines playing cards with Bill Byrnes in Sonora. He lights a cigar in the last of the dying embers. He sees the sun rising high above the Sierra and watches *vaqueros* riding toward the pastures. He passes them and tips his hat. His aging legs throw his horse into a lope through the hills toward the valley, toward hunger, toward wandering, and toward an uncertain end.

—————◆◆◆◆◆—————

—*Steven McFann is a writer born and raised in California. His lifelong pas-*

sion for the history of the American West was sparked by childhood visits to the Autry Museum, his teenage love for the work of Sergio Leone and Clint Eastwood, and the western-inspired art of his uncle Gary McFann, as well as the art of his grandfather's cousin, celebrated western artist Don Crowley. His work has appeared in Saddlebag Dispatches, Empyrean Literary Magazine, *and the entertainment website ScreenRant. He is also the author of the Substack blog "Fool's Gold," which details the history of California from the Gold Rush to WWI. Counting the likes of James Ellroy, Cormac McCarthy, Michel Houllebecq, Hubert Selby Jr, and Larry McMurtry as his influences, he is currently working on two novels and a screenplay. When not writing or working as a stagehand, he loves reading, listening to music, and exploring the southwest's majestic deserts.*

Pierre by Alfred Jacob Miller

THE
SLOW GO QUICK
BLANCHE DESCHAIN

TO SHERIFF ROY Munroe, the sheets snapping in the wind look like old yellowed shrouds. Some linens have fallen into the dirt, where they lie, dusty and limp, against the boards of a porch. The only sounds—the steady moan of the wind and a metallic squeal coming from somewhere further into town. No dogs bark in alarm at their arrival, no smoke drifts from chimneys, the town is silent as a burying yard.

The sun hangs low in the sky, glowering and red. True summer's heat is not upon the land, but a wind, hot as a baking oven, has started to blow up from the south. Roy looks over his shoulder at his companion, Cooper, squinting against the sun. He leans to spit over his boot into the dust that billows up as they ride. They both cluck to their horses, pulling them to a more cautious pace. They have reached the first of the buildings.

With a jarring clap a mass of black birds rise from the street beyond, wings snapping louder than the sheet-shrouds. A wake of large, ungainly bodies, flap heavily onto the rooftops, dislodging a few tattered feathers, to watch them pass. Cooper's gelding gives a nervous snort at the scent of blood and loose guts that hits them with a shift of the wind.

Journeying a little farther in, they find why the dogs aren't barking. Affixed to one of the batwing doors of the saloon is a black-and-white sheepdog. Beside the rough-timber building, a small windmill turns, the metal squealing as the wind pushes the rust-flecked blades. Tied to the windmill looks to be a severed paw of a large cat, held with a bit of leather tack.

The paw drags softly through the dirt, twisting slowly in the wind.

In the dust nearby, a pair of legs sprawl from a rumpled heap of petticoats. Roy hitches his buckskin in front of the saloon. He spits over the toe of his boot, slowly taking in what passes for a town square. Cooper grunts and draws his eyes to an untouched pie that rests on a window ledge, between a pair of fluttering curtains.

Both men slide down from the saddle, sending up sprays of sulfur-yellow dust around their boots. Roy grabs a rifle from his saddle and checks his Colt. He heads toward the doors, seeing the dog is pinned there by a tomahawk. He pulls it free, blood clotted hard to the handle. Flies buzz up around him when the body is freed, angry and loud as a plague.

He surveys the weapon pinning the poor creature. It seems to be from the Pawnee nearby, but Roy doubts it was them who had done this. The other threat close by, a group he knew had disagreements with the town in the past, was the Mormon settlers. Since arriving here years ago, they'd been at odds with every living thing ever since. Roy doesn't figure it was them either.

He uses a dusty boot to flip the woman, in her ruffle of petticoats, over, and another vengeful cloud of flies billows up. Her blue eyes are wide open, dark bruises ring her throat. Her head is canted at a disturbing angle. She looks shocked at her death, and Roy closes her eyes with a calloused hand.

Inside the saloon, the light is dim with the dust filtering through chinks in the rafters. Some of the tables are overturned, legs splintered. His leather boots crunch as he moves through the glass that litters the floor. The huge mirror behind the bar, one that would have cost a lifetime of wages for the people in this town, is partly shattered.

Roy had bent an elbow at this bar many times, over the long years, on his way to other trails. Jay, the bartender and owner of the bar, had been proud of that mirror. He'd liked to tell a long story about how it had been brought by the steamboat *Nina Tilden* down the Colorado River, years back. Roy thinks the dead woman outside must be his oldest daughter, Alice. She had been learning to tend bar last time he visited.

Behind the bar he spots Jay, bloated and cold as a wagon tire, a Winchester clutched in his hands. His eyes are staring sightless at the shattered mirror above him. Roy places a bar cloth across the man's face. With a grunt, he pries the rifle from the man's hands.

Cooper waits for him in the dust of the yard. They find the rest of the town in the same state of butchery. Wanton destruction, the only way Roy can find to name it. It's impossible to tell how many riders had descended upon the town, but there had been a good fifteen families living here. They found no survivors.

In a lean-to, they find some of the livestock, lying in puddles of gore. There weren't enough beasts to maintain all the families, and Roy figures the raiders must have taken the livestock when they were done. He reckons there will be little chance they'll be able to track on this dry, parched soil.

Both men hear the sound of hooves, hands going to their guns on long-lived instinct. Dust billows up as five riders pull horses to a stop outside the saloon. In silence, they jump down and tie their horses alongside the rail. The men gather in the dust of the square as the last, hot rays of sun vanish below the horizon.

"We searched. Didn't find nobody alive," one man rumbles, pulling a flask from a pocket with dirt-rimmed fingers.

Roy clears his throat and spits, his mind mulling over the task. He directs the men to head into town to begin pulling the bodies into the streets. These men are named deputies who help for a fee, most of them good men. He trusts them to not loot the bodies while he can see.

As he passes down the line, counting bodies, they are starting to stink something fierce now. His men load them into a wagon. The townsfolk will be carried out onto the hard-pack and buried as deep as they can manage in the dust.

Honestly, he can't figure who would have done this. A massacre like this doesn't usually happen just once. Some men are just wolves in man-skin, they can't leave it alone once they've had their taste of blood. He shakes his head to clear it of too much rumination. Clearing his throat, he hawks into the dirt beside his boots. Running a hand over his weather-tanned face, he replaces his hat, and goes to supervise the burial.

<hr>

NINETEEN YEARS AGO

ONCE A MAN rode out of the badlands and stole a young girl from the yard before her family's cabin. In bondage for fifteen years, the girl grew to a woman, and she bore a son to the man that took her. The man was a trapper, ridden down from the cold North. He lived a hard life, competing with the land and its beasts.

The woman not only survived but gained skill as a trapper herself. She earned her own horse and a bit of freedom from the hard side of the man's fist. One day, instead of clearing traps, she took her son and rode out for the home she remembered. Planning well, she'd cached food and supplies along her route and returned with her young son to a joyous reunion with her family.

Despite the happy arrival, the woman and her son were never fully accepted back. Her parents didn't quite know what to do with her. They knew even less what to do with her wild-eyed son. She remarried and started back to church on Sunday's. She had two children by her new husband and settled into life as a staid matron. Despite her best efforts, her eldest son always kept the rage of the wild inside him. Everyone was uneasy around the boy.

As a small child, he pushed his siblings into the dirt with a delighted laugh. He found a certain joy in tormenting the nanny goats and pulling the dog's tail that he did not find in common child's play. As he got older, his behavior became more volatile. One summer, a fight over a puppy ended when he broke his half-brother's arm. Rather than take a whipping, he tore the belt from his stepfather's hand and turned leather on the old man. The boy saw his mother's silent tears, but she did not come to him this time. He ran from his home into the wilds.

Only, a week later found him returned, bored of being alone. He stared from the edge of the yard as night settled on the log-chink house. His mother sobbed to see him, mad-eyed and barefoot in the dark. Before dawn the next day, she took him to a nearby town and tucked him into a hired coach. The boy was sent to live with her brother who resided on the outskirts of San Diego.

Upon arrival the boy took a deep dislike to his uncle. His uncle's skinny, weasel-like manner and wilted mustache seemed unmanly to the boy. Added to this was his uncle's enthusiastic love for *aguardiente*.

This habit disgusted the boy. The smell of black licorice soon drove him to madness. In retaliation, the boy began to hurt the hunting dogs when his uncle was sleeping. The uncle was no fighter and began to fear him. He resolved to rid himself of the boy with haste.

From his uncle's, he was sent to an acquaintance who managed a blacksmith shop. The uncle hoped the physical labor would tire out the boy's devil-temper and, after the transfer, washed his hands of the matter. Before a week had passed, the boy grew angry and shoved the blacksmith into a pan of smelted ore. The man ran screaming into the street cursing the boy's name to the heavens. The smell of steaming molten-flesh and metal filled the air.

Pouring from doors, the townsfolk had beaten the boy and rode him out on a rail, dumping him bloody into the dust. His exile from humanity, and his separation from any rational sense of mercy, was complete as he nursed his bruises and shattered ribs in the desert. He returned by night to the blacksmith's town and slit the throat of all the dogs before dumping their bodies into the well. Stealing the blacksmith's horse was a final insult. He returned to the wilds, the place he now considered his home.

He returned to the plains and took to stealing horses, knocking over the occasional stagecoach, when the opportunity presented itself. By his sixteenth birthday, he looked like a full-grown man. He was alone for now, and bored. He had been watching a farm for the last few days. To his sight, there was a small woman in a blue-homespun dress and her young son living alone. He'd seen no men around, and the woman rarely carried a rifle. The farm had quite a few buckskins in pasture and a white-washed barn full of clean hay and well-fed horseflesh.

The boy had fallen asleep that morning, the hot sun closing his eyes, in the dappled shade beneath the trees. While asleep, he missed the arrival of a hulking figure, hat pulled low and six-gun shining. Securing a gelding in the barn, the giant had gone into the woman and her son.

That night, he walked to the barn, whistling. He had no fear of a woman and child. He earned himself a bite, trying to place a halter on the nicest piece of horseflesh in the barn. Distracted by the struggling horse, he didn't hear the gun cock behind him until it was too late to react.

"Turn around slow, son," a gravelly voice spoke the words like a pronouncement, the words heavy with menace.

The boy turned slowly, hands up and spread, to see a giant of a woman, thick-muscled, with sun-tanned skin and a wicked scar over her eye. Her face was puffy with sleep, but her hand steady as rock holding the large revolver pointed dead at the boy's eye.

"Explain what you are doing," the woman said into the quiet of the horse-scented barn. The anxious horse had stilled to gentleness at her presence.

Nervous for some reason he couldn't name, the boy shifted his weight. The woman narrowed her eyes at his movement, and the boy stilled himself quickly. After an uncomfortable long moment of silence, the woman lowered the gun. After a good look-over, the woman dismissed him, muscles relaxing. She did not see him as a threat. The boy found himself more curious than angry at this fact. When the woman began to talk, the boy listened. He learned that her name was Sheridan. She was visiting her sister on her farm today, lucky for them all, she supposed.

Her sister's husband died a few weeks back. Sheridan had come to stay with her to help keep the farm going. After their talk in the barn, she invited him to stay, as well. He earned his keep chopping wood and fetching water. At her side, he learned to mend tack and clean hooves.

On the day, Sheridan saw for herself the boy's darkness, she was afraid for perhaps the first time in her life. Coming back early from a visit to a neighbor, she found the boy had pinned her sister's son to the ground and beaten him bloody. She'd taken the limp-bodied child in to her sister, keeping one eye on the boy shuffling his feet in the yard. When asked, the boy couldn't explain why he'd done it.

Sheridan had taken him on a ride to the prairie then. They'd both dismounted in the waist high grass. When she asked a third time and the boy gave no answer, she decked him with a hard right-hook across the jaw. They fought then, long and hard. Blood splattered across the grass beneath them as they battled. Eventually, Sheridan got the upper hand and pinned the boy.

Even still, the boy fought like a demon, well past the point he'd dislocated his arm, Sheridan felt queasy at the pop of bone. All the while, he refused to give out a whimper. He looked like a rabid dog, panting there in the dust, covered in the blood and spit of their brawl. After that day, she took the boy firmly under her wing and tried to teach him right from wrong.

PRESENT DAY

SHERIDAN WOKE FROM a deep, murky sleep. She wearily swam up from the depths of whiskey, wondering, not for the first time, how she didn't drown for good. Her mouth tasted foul and she leaned to hawk out the dusty window by her bed. Her union suit was threadbare, yellowed with too much wear and not enough washing. Carefully, she lit the stump of a wet cigar, pulled from a puddle of spilled hooch, and she inhaled with relief.

She made her way to the door, where someone had been insistently pounding. Leaning against the door she coughed and rubbed her chest with a broad, callused hand. Sleeping in a damp attic room above a poker parlor wasn't easy on the lungs. Grumbling, she rubbed her knee. She wondered at why it ached, now that she'd got some years on her.

Pulling open the door, Sheridan squinted, her vision a bit fuzzy around the edges these last years. Two familiar men stood there, Roy and Cooper, trail companions from years ago. She groaned at the bright bars of late sunlight that filled the hallway behind them. She stumbled back onto the sagging mattress. Roy took the rickety stool by the window. He handed her a dented flask, and she took it gratefully. The liquor helped clear her head enough to listen to the story he had brought her.

Roy explained what happened in the dead town. For months, he and Cooper had been trying to track the ones who did it. Sheridan wondered what this had to do with her. She'd retired from bounty hunting long ago. Roy saw the refusal on her face. Looking away from her eyes, he almost seemed embarrassed. He pulled out a much-folded piece of paper and handed it to her. Sheridan unfolded the paper and felt her heart crack.

She took another deep swig of the flask, feeling the edge of the shakes creeping up despite it all. It was the boy's face there, *her* boy, but hard and lean now. No trace of boyhood was left in him. He had his own scar now, too, running from right below his eye down to the corner of his lip. That scar pulled his face up into a sneer. Roy told her how the boy'd been killing his way across the land. They couldn't stop him. She heard the fear behind his words.

The boy left a trademark behind, a tawny cat's paw, every place he'd murdered his way through. Roy said they'd tracked him across two states, and was a ghost to them. Sheridan thought back to all she'd taught him and realized they wouldn't be able to catch him. She had a deep-set cough now. Riding would be hard on her old bones. She also knew this was her job. It always had been. She drank more of the whiskey. Finally, she handed the empty flask back to Roy.

"We ride in a quarter hour," she grunted, waving them out the door.

After she splashed her face with the tepid water on the washstand and forced herself to eat some of the cold chicken left from dinner, she felt better. She put on a clean shirt and pulled her short-laced boots up, rubbing at her stiff knee. Her knuckles were swollen with age. Her belly felt full of lead shot, but a feeling she thought long-lost was stirring in her. Outside, there's a saddled horse waiting for her, and they rode out.

Three weeks hard riding and the rumors of the raiders led them to a box canyon in the Arizona desert. Inside the canyon, the air smelled of sage and old death. They found the remains of five dead men and two women. The bodies sprawled in their bedding.

A mountain lion's paw dangled from a post driven into the sandy ground beside the campfire's ashes. Sheridan surveyed the scene with a deep ache of sadness growing under her breastbone. She should have taken care of the boy, long ago, when she first found out he had something wrong with him.

Having found the majority of those they seek for bounties, Roy and Cooper turned back. They were too far from home with too small a crew to go after a madman like this deep in the wilds. They urged Sheridan to return with them, Roy not saying outright that he was worried for her, but she could sense it. No matter, she was resolute in her pursuit. Sheridan never gave up a trail before. She wouldn't do it on what may be her final one. She continued on by herself, knowing she moved closer to a destiny long denied.

In Mexico, Sheridan finally got sure word of the boy—heard that he was living in the next town over. From what she can gather, he'd not done any hard killings since crossing the border. Rumor was the boy even dispatched a band of horse thieves that was troubling the nearby road. Forming a posse with some of the young sons of nearby ranchers, he'd led them all to dispatch the attackers and then safely home after.

The moon was full when Sheridan finally arrived at the rolling fields of a cattle ranch. She silently cursed her choice to arrive at night, damning her failing vision. She wasn't being as careful as she would have been years ago, and she damned herself for that as well.

She was sure of herself earlier, when she had called at the house and asked for the boy. At the door, a nervous young woman directed her to this field. The boy stepped quietly from the shadows, spooking her horse. He broke into a grin, now slightly marred by the scar that stretched his cheek. He didn't look surprised to see her still alive. Sheridan dismounted, looking the boy over—careful to keep her hand away from iron. She decided he didn't look much changed from when he stood over her last.

The boy told her that he married the daughter of the rancher and now the owner of the cattle before them. Sheridan walked her horse back to the ranch for breakfast with him. She listened as her boy told her about his life without her. She noted he left out the razing of the towns and the slaughter of his gang.

At the ranch house, the boy introduced his wife. A young, slight woman with black sloe-eyes set in a heart-shaped face. Showing her to a well-polished table, he poured them a fine whiskey from a cut-glass carafe, probably the finest Sheridan had tasted. Later that night, Sheridan was directed to a handsome room with a crackling fire with a fine bed and a soft quilt.

It was deep night when something woke Sheridan in that warm bed, beneath that fine quilt. At first, she wasn't sure why she woke up. Then, suddenly, she knew the boy was there in the darkness, a shadow from hell itself. She felt the cold press of a gun barrel against her temple. Some deep part of her sighed in relief, that it was about to be over, and she didn't have to put him down. It would be easier on her this way.

She hoped her father would not be disappointed in her. She watched him, unable to see his eyes. She felt the pressure of the barrel leave as he lowered the gun. He ghosted out of the open door without speaking. Sheridan wondered if she'd pissed herself. She was glad when she found out she hadn't.

Lying there, watching the flames dance in the fireplace, she thought back to the days when she tried to teach the boy to do right. Tried to teach him to turn from the darkness in himself. She had taught the boy as her father, Pat, had taught her. Her father had been a kind man, but stern. He taught her how to read the weather, live in the wilds, to track men, and hunt and butcher game.

Her father had also expertly instilled in her the ideals of good and evil. Sheridan firmly believed evil should not be allowed to triumph. She in turn, had tried to instill all this morality in the boy.

Things went on well enough between Sheridan and the boy for a while. He rode shotgun and seemed to learn from her. It was just turning winter, a bitter cold day, when things went bad. They had hired on to a wealthy family, returning a woman safely to her kin, from a marriage gone bad. They'd ended up in a shootout that killed the husband, him full as a tick on liquor and shotgun happy. In high-spirits, they'd returned to their camp with the grateful woman.

Sheridan had come back from refilling her water-skin to find the boy defiling the woman. She'd taken a blow to the head that was already swelling her face. Sheridan flew from her horse in a rage and knocked him away from the woman. She drew back a fist, intending to give him the deepest thrashing of his life, unsure if she'd let him live after this or not.

Quick as a snake striking, the boy pulled out the gun Sheridan herself had given him, and shot her dead in the gut. Shot her in a way nobody should shoot a dog. Then he left her to die. Sheridan lost consciousness, staring up into the gray sky, flecks of snow just beginning to dust her wind-chapped face.

When she came to, she found the woman cold dead by the ashes of the fire. He was long gone with the horses and gear. Sheridan lost herself to darkness again, as pain swamped her, a part of her hoping she did not wake again.

She did wake, many hours later, in what seemed like a fever dream. Forcing her eyes to focus, she saw an ancient woman bent over her. Black eyes and a deeply wrinkled face, surrounded by a halo of white hair. At times, Sheridan awoke to see a hawk sitting across the fire, watching her intently with golden-moon eyes.

One night Sheridan woke, feeling a rare moment of lucidity. Embers spun up from a tall fire, the old woman was muttering to herself, words Sheridan didn't know. She felt the heat from the fire, baking her, or perhaps that was the fever that wracked her body. Sometimes it felt as if the bullet wound had its own heartbeat, pounding, so loud, it drowned out her own heart. She wanted to ask the woman why she was helping her, but her throat was burning, cracked like clay.

Looking up, the old woman saw she was awake. Lifting her head with surprisingly strong, but gnarled fingers, she tipped a bitter, herbal-mixture into Sheridan's mouth. She wondered if she wanted something from her. Couldn't she see there's nothing here but a dead woman?

A knot popped in the fire and Sheridan's eyes shifted toward it. When she looked back, a hawk was sitting beside the old woman, on a woven blanket. Sheridan blinked in surprise but stayed silent.

"I am making you a trade. I need nothing from you, for free, woman." The old woman paused, Sheridan sensed bitterness beneath her silence. Finally, the ageless-ancient woman took a breath and smoothed her wrinkled face clear of emotion.

"Tonight, I give you a life. You may live it as you will. Only, when you are done with that life, you will put down a beast that threatens my blood." She held up a withered, bird-boned hand to still the questions that threatened to spill from Sheridan.

"Until then, you will live under the shadow of this day. In the end, it will be a relief." The woman waved a hand vaguely at her wound, her fever, at the immense pain that rocked Sheridan's body with chills.

Sheridan lived, just like the old woman said she would, and she was grateful. But something inside her shattered and stayed broken from that day. A part of her had always known she'd have to face the boy again. She blew out a long sigh and settled back beneath the quilt to wait for daybreak.

The morning dawned red as blood. A storm boiled up from the west. The smell of lightning was in the air. A cold-wind slammed dust and small stones hard against her skin. She waited on the porch and the young wife joined her. Together they watched the steel-gray thunderheads rolling in.

The pair stood against the wind, old woman and young, the silence broken only by the whistle of a hawk. There was a sharp snap of wings as it took a mouse from beneath the porch rail at their feet.

The boy joined them on the splintered porch and Sheridan clapped a hand to his shoulder. Together they walked into the ripe grass. She felt oddly at peace then. Fondly, she remembered walking with him on the prairie, when they were both younger. When the world was younger. They stood watching the storm close in above them. The rain started to sheet down in the distance, iron-walls of rain billowed toward them.

Giving the boy no warning, Sheridan suddenly uncoiled from her relaxed stance, releasing the tightly held tension that had been thrumming through her body for weeks. She threw a punch as good as any in her youth, a hard right hook for the history books. His head snapped back as she landed the blow. Without pause, she followed up with another that knocked three teeth from his jaw.

The boy was confused by her sudden attack, a quicksilver flash of fear in his eyes. His nose sheeted blood down his front. The rain hit them then, like a blow, plastering hair and clothing flat. His hand slipped on the hilt of the knife as he tried to pull it from the buckskin sheath. He wasn't ready for an attack like this. In the past, she had always been so steady, so merciful. Sheridan knocked another fist deep into his gut, driving him back to his knees. She brought up her fist for another right hook and the boy brought his knife up to meet her.

He sunk the knife deep into her gut, right in the place he'd put a bullet in her years before. The pain of it distant, she brushed it aside. As the boy ripped the knife free, she saw blood jet from her belly. A feral light filled the boy's eyes, pupils blown, teeth bared in a death's-head grin. He raised his knife again.

She brought her own knife up instead. Right under his ribs, she sunk the blade neatly into his heart. The way it should've done, the way she'd tried to show him. A simple, quick blow, to put a suffering creature out of pain. She held him to her broad chest while the fight went out of his eyes.

Sheridan considered the ranch house in the distance, the family inside. She thought of walking to them for help. She laid down beside the boy in the tall grass. She let her old bones rest.

—*Blanche Deschain writes books about the women that live inside her barbarous mind. Strong, strapping women, fox-clever females, hero-women that step in when the world has become too wild. Her passion for the west was ignited when she moved to Utah to live with her grandmother, an avid genealogist. This wise-woman imparted a love and a passion for giving life to the stories we tell ourselves.*

Blanche also writes poetry about the spirituality, religion and darkness that inhabits the red-earth of the deep south. She has a poetry book titled Bury Me in the Red Clay. *Her poetry was also published in the first volume of* Carolina Muse, *a publication in Chapel Hill, NC. She also has an Instagram account for poetry @bluebeardbeldame.*

Before she started writing short stories and poetry, Blanche got a Bachelors in Zoology and Plant Biology from NC State University. After that, just to see how the cat jumped, she worked as a 911 dispatcher and a wildlife rescuer. She is a jewelry maker, baker, herbalist, and witch in her spare time. She currently resides on Vancouver Island with her husband and daughter.

MOUNTAIN MAIL RUNNER FEBRUARY 1859

MOSS SPRINGMEYER

THE CALIFORNIA GOLD Rush of 1849 dragged Jack west willy-nilly like a magnet seizing an iron filing. Thousands of other iron filings were tumbled along too, jolted loose from their pasts, a brotherhood of zest for adventure and dazzling dreams of riches. He'd chased every whisper of a gold strike for five years. Some whispers were will-o'-the-wisps. Others were real, but luck was not with him. Time for a change. One thing was sure. He'd learnt to live rough, and he was going to stay in the West.

Then, one night in the saloon, the Mica, California postmaster said he hadn't laid eyes on Long Tom, the mail runner, since Tom snowshoed up the Emigrant Trail toward Beckworth Meadows three weeks before. The recent blizzard had likely killed him on the way back. Jack had jumped at the job. Later, he'd learnt the skills to carry it out.

He'd begun by stumbling, tripping, and falling in the heavy wooden snowshoes, called "rackets" for their likeness to tennis gear. The first dozen tumbles taught him that he couldn't just charge through, a humbling lesson for a man so tall and strong. He'd tried taking longer and shorter strides, raising his legs higher and lower, swinging the rackets wide and narrow. The first attempts with the high lift, left the front of his thighs burning and swollen the next morning. Trying out the wide swings planted pain lurking to shoot up the insides of his thighs at the slightest sideways motion the next day. But those muscles grew strong and supple, high lift and wide swing became second nature.

The pinch of magic that pulled it together was a bounce. As each step landed, he bounced a little, giving the opposite leg an extra lift just as it started to swing forward. That cured the stumbling. Breathing an explosive "Ha!" aloud every other step recruited the gut muscles to the heave and helped him find the rhythm.

The snowshoe struggle became the racket dance. It was still hard work, but joyful, too. That little bounce lifted his heart as well as his snowshoe. Out on his own, he'd quack now and then, just for the hell of it, imagining himself a long-legged duck waddling up the trail.

Now, after a week in town, too many card games and too much booze, Jack welcomed his mail-route routine. Five years had engraved it into his soul, but it was always a new adventure. At the snowline, he hopped off the Mica mail wagon and gulped the astringent tang of the pines. He scooped up his fur blanket roll, satchel, and snowshoes. Another dive into the wagon brought up a bundle of poles and a frame crisscrossed with rawhide mesh which he would assemble into a travois. Using the travois, he would move that huge mail sack, three times as much as he could have carried on his back. Lastly, he manhandled out the 200-pound waxed-canvas sack. He'd be taking it east up the Emigrant Trail over the towering Tormentoso Range through Swayback Pass and down to his friends and neighbors at the Fort Hotel in Beckworth Meadows.

He imagined the sack squirming with colorful living threads eager to connect far flung family and friends with the Beckworth Meadows folks. A letter hectoring the orphaned apprentice-lawyer to be born again would warm the boy with his uncle's love. The cutler would hear his sweetheart whisper of the stirrings of spring in South Carolina. The ranching trio of brothers would read into their father's wearisome tirade on states' rights, his unspoken care and worries about their safety. The inn keeper would read the illiterates their letters. Their little community would hum with connections.

The mail wagon, the last wheels he'd hear until his return, rolled away with the usual hearty "Better you than me! Good luck!" The next human voices would be happy shouts greeting him and the mail at the Fort Hotel. Now, the silence was torn only by the harsh caws of the blue jays, the tinkling trills of the juncos, and the diminutive cacophony of "chick-a-dee-dee-dees" darting and fluttering past. Behind it all, the susurration of the perpetual breeze in the pine tops, a sound so native to the mountain realm that it whispered below awareness.

The alpine sounds lifted his spirit as he worked, lashing the travois's two long poles onto a cross-piece just wider than his shoulders. He then tied the frame between the poles' other ends, the whole looking like an A-frame ladder. The mail would ride on the mesh-covered frame. He would push against the cross-piece with his chest, dragging the back ends along the snow, knee-high powder resting on packed snow deeper than three men standing on each other's shoulders.

He strove up the track into the green and white solitude, so familiar, but never the same. He thought, "I'm an otter back in the water. I'm a hawk climbing the sky!" Every muscle sang, strong and elastic, an ecstasy of motion.

As the sun sank behind him, the pines' pointed shadows stretched into spearheads, obsidian on the sparkling snow. He smiled that they pointed his way eastward up the Emigrant Trail, the shortest route to his base at the Fort Hotel. The surface powder he toiled through would be three or even four feet deep before he reached Swayback Pass, seventy miles ahead and 9,500 feet high, the lowest dip in the Sierra Tormentoso's crest for miles. Until spring, the steep snow-swathed slopes banished hooved animals. Even the deer wintered in the valleys.

———————————◆◆◆◆◆◆———————————

THE THIRD DAY brought Jack to Swayback Pass. The juncos stayed lower down, but up here at the edge of the sky, chickadee troupes chittered and swooped and jay caws boasted and argued. No matter how many times he came, the sheer wonder of this between-land cleansed his soul. What a miracle to be walking yards above the ground that was itself almost two miles in the sky, with the majestic peaks soaring even higher both south and north of the pass. Past his long climb up the west slope, but not yet into the steep descent down the east side, he sped across the flat, his motion fluid, almost effortless.

There was something otherworldly about the pass, he thought, as though whatever was making the mountains had come roaring up from the south, paused to catch its breath here, and then raged on, rending and ripping and roaring north. An alien being, magnificent, hugely powerful, dangerously indifferent.

The blood sang in his veins, and his whole body rejoiced as he danced east across the level pass. For a blissful moment, his starting point and his destination did not matter, he was in the landscape and of the landscape, and it was in him and of him.

Was that moment what heaven was like? Could a human soul bear it for long? He began to feel more separate again, still joyful, but more distinct. The crisply focused view before him ended abruptly five miles ahead. In the distance rose vaguer mountain ranges, flat like torn paper, the nearer ones dark, the furthest almost as pale as the lavender of the fading day. Below sight, in the gap between the end of the immediate crisp view and the nearest of the paper cutout ranges, at the foot of the Tormentoso lay his goal. The glorious solitude, the floating feeling of awe subsided as the homey prospect of arrival arose.

Each stride drew him closer to flinging wide the Fort Hotel's front door to devour the savory aromas of venison stew and fresh bread. Friends and neighbors would jostle for his news and smile that he had made it again– glad to share the victory, because they all knew that crossing the Tormentoso in winter was dueling with Death. That fellowship would gladden their hearts, feeling a little bit stronger when he was with them. And how the mail would rejoice them, renewing and strengthening their ties to absent friends and loved ones.

Catching a strange fresh whiff, the warning perfume announcing a storm, he thrust on faster. The bright blue sky went white.

The cold sharpened till he could no longer smell the pines. Their murmur deepened to a growl. Up here, the snowpack rose so high that he looked into the midriffs of the trees– underneath the powder, the snow surface was solid, yet higher than a man on stilts.

The wind pushed harder and deeper into the forest, filling and erupting where, moments before, chickadee calls had trilled. The little hairs inside his nose froze together, tickling and tugging at his nostrils.

Feathery flakes gave way to a fast, dense, swirling snow, disguising his way. Pushing against the wind was devouring his zest and strength. His alertness shifted into alarm. The storm is taking too much out of me, he thought.

Even the jays hushed and hid. The wind roared and whipped from everywhere at once, stinging the bare skin around his eyes. Deeply thankful for the thick furs protecting him everywhere else, he went on.

Not going to be an everyday storm. Got to get the mail through some-how, he thought, pushing down the fear. He let himself imagine those colorful, living filaments of connection, reaching from everywhere through his mail sack to the people awaiting them.

He squinted against the driving snow. The lashes in his eyes' outer corners began to freeze together so he popped his lids wide every few strides. But at the same time, the sting of the snow on his eyes triggered the lids to close. The snow surface on which he strode and the white sky merged into one close yet limitless blurry envelopment. I'm in the cloud now, he thought. In this alien white world, if he should stray, the familiar pines and rocks were so changed by the heavy snow and the sculpting wind that he might not find his way back.

The storm verged on blizzard and his hope flattened. Pitted against the storm, a dull ache in his thighs was ramping up. The muscle knot between his shoulder blades was cramping. How long could he fight the wind as well as normal exhaustion? Fear began to tingle outward through his muscles to his fingertips and toes. The mail runner before him wasn't the only man who had died in such a storm. He'd heard of people bewildered by a blizzard losing their way between their cabin and their barn, frozen to death just steps from their safe, warm kitchens. Smart folks put up a guide rope to follow between barn and homestead. There'd be no guide here. Grim determination was carrying him. "No!" he shouted, "I will not die!"

The wind roared louder and drove the snow stinging hard from every which way. The *travois* dragged heavier and heavier. Luckily it was low-slung, it did not catch much wind. Usually, somewhere near this point he could camp, but today the wind and the snow and the arctic cold would freeze anyone camping.

He strode on, his load heavier and heavier, laboring through the wind and deepening powder, guessing how far he had come. He could shovel out a snow shelter using his rackets, but he'd heard of people smothering in them. The Simpsons' abandoned cabin should be pretty close. He squinted and blinked into the snow, peering for the lightning-blasted tree that would mark the path to the cabin.

The flying snow seemed somehow both solid and intangible. When he shoved it aside, swiping a clear spot in front of his eyes, it did not resist. But the space filled even before he finished the gesture. *Like wrestling with a phantom,* he thought. As he strove forward, panting displaced the deep even breathing that had steadied and accelerated his strides in the racket dance. He tried to recover the rhythmic breathing, but slipped back into panting whenever his thoughts drifted. Exhaustion extinguished the bounce in his stride. His thigh and rump muscles were shooting pain, his shoulders and back throbbing. Disorientation flashed. The heavy *travois* hindered him, demanding a ponderous struggle as the powder drifted, and the wind shoved and pushed him and battered him with noise.

Just when he needed the smooth swift motion most, all he could conjure was laborious lumbering. Then he wobbled. Could his muscles be failing? *No!*

Damn you, Mother Nature! he thought. Then *Damn me! Cocksure that I knew every one of your twists and turns!*

Energy spurted through him, reviving the racket dance for another hundred yards. Then the bounce vanished again, and he could not ignore the pain. He clenched his fists, punching with each stride. Maybe if he sat down, just for a minute, strength would flow back into him. No. He toiled on, gritting his teeth, clinging to the image of the glowing living filaments running through his mail sack, connecting his community to their far flung kin.

Could he have missed the scorched tree? The huge poles of the lower trunks of the pines were buried in snow. He slogged through an amputated forest of branch-clad middles and tapering tops, mostly white but shadow-smudged and accented in green. Snow-swaddled trees materialized out of the swirling white as he passed—now and then one brushing his shoulder, behind them ranks and ranks dwindling and melding into the encompassing white of snow and cloud. Maybe he hadn't come as far as he thought. His gut knotted. If he should fall, he would be done. Suppose he was lost and didn't know it. A moment of vertigo left him uneasy, not confident about which way was up.

From the smothering-thick snow on his right, a man-sized dark smear emerged and took shape as the lighting-blasted tree. He wept and filled his lungs as he turned down the path, praising the builders of the cabin, constructed of logs discarded from clearing the Track. The snow whirled. Nearly blinded, on an ax's edge between hard-won caution and desperate haste, he slogged toward the cabin. A few more clumsy steps and he crashed into the log wall.

He loosed the straps and kicked off his snowshoes to dig out the door. The struggle to see beyond the relentless pain in his legs and torso was making him giddy. The luxurious pull of doing nothing tugged at him again and again, inviting him to take a break, rest his back against a tree, and let go. No. He accepted the near-death weariness and held firmly in mind the haven awaiting him. Shelter was within reach and people were counting on him. Those letters would renew and strengthen the threads of love, connecting the Beckworth Meadows ranchers and prospectors and even the ne'er-do-wells to their fathers and mothers, sisters and brothers, friends and lovers back East. It was up to him.

He began by flinging the snow far aside. The deeper he dug, the harder the work. Not only was the lower snow densely packed by the sheer weight above, but he also had to lift these deeper loads higher.

He took for granted that his arms, shoulder, and back would answer his call to lift, but suddenly, they did not. He tried once more, but got nothing. Betrayal. Rage.

Rejecting the rising panic, he inhaled deeply, inflating his entire torso, accepting the pause, and looking past it to a vision of stepping through the door, into a still space with log walls deflecting the battering, roaring wind. Another deep breath and, yes, this time the body answered. But could he trust it? Very deliberately now, breathing and shoveling.

At last, the door gaped. He hauled his gear through and collapsed into the stillness of the shack. Safe, at last. His muscles suddenly slack. Shelter, haven, rest. He sprawled beside the door, weeping.

Spent, he focused on unfurling his hands, near-frozen into curving claws, now the numbness pierced by a riot of sensation mingling intense tingling with a sudden burning. The wind raged on outside.

As his eyes adjusted to the gloom, a darker piece of darkness took shape below the rafter. It looked almost like, and was, a man, a hanged man. Fighting the impulse to flee, Jack lurched up and staggered over. But the hanged man was cold and no pulse pumped through his wrist. Up close, Jack glimpsed a face distorted into a grotesque parody, a carnival mask. He almost screamed with disgust. Was that a fat snake hanging out of the mouth? No, it was just a tongue bloated huge with blood and the muscle gone slack after death.

Nausea rose, but extreme fatigue overwhelmed it. He stumbled back, loosed the fur blanket from the *travois,* collapsed on the mail sack, and nestled into it. He forced himself to eat some pemmican, the frontier traveler's compound of fat, berries, and jerky. Then, settling the heavy fur over him demanded concentration. Exhaustion had exacted its price, his fingers were slow, his grip clumsy, he felt tipsy. Nonetheless, by habit and sheer determination, he arranged his clothing and the blanket to be as warm as possible–any exposed skin would freeze in the night.

A surge of horror at the hanged man thrust Jack up. Pause. He swayed. He knew that the blizzard promised death, so he must stay. Yet, the prospect of spending the night with the corpse spurred him to flee. In his delirium of exhaustion, an image of the friendly gathering in the warmth of the Fort Hotel came to him, and an insidious voice urged that hurrying away to summon help would honor the dead. He yearned to say, "Yes," but recognized the shimmer of falsity at the edges from past experience of tempting mirages of water in the Boneyard Desert. He recoiled.

He pushed the horror down, reminding himself that he had seen dead men before and that he had a job to do. But the dead men he had seen had died in accidents or simple violence. No face had ever looked like this. The horror stirred like a rabid bear in the cellar, but he kept it trapped. Being himself trapped in the shack made that hard. He focused on what he must do on the morrow, but his thoughts kept circling back to the hanged man. Who was he? Why had he hanged himself? Why here?

Subsiding, Jack nestled back into the mailbag. His mind reached for the blissful awe he had felt as he entered the pass, but he could not find it. As his eyes closed, he welcomed an imaginary guide rope–homemade cordage like his Beckworth Meadows friends fashioned–he could follow to the Fort Hotel. His focus shifted so the guide rope shrank to a tiny cord in a bird's-eye vision of the whole country with brightly colored, living threads stretching into the mail sack—short ones reaching east from California, long ones fanning out east, south to the Carolinas, and north to Maine. It was up to him to keep those threads alive.

Sleep began as delicious, complete rest.

Then he found himself a mute, invisible, paralyzed, anguished observer. He watched the dream stranger clench his jaw, carefully knot the noose, climb a ladder to tie the rope onto the rafter, then descend weeping, fetch a tall, sturdy wooden stool, step onto it, and check the length of the rope. The dream stranger then shortened the rope, dragged the noose over his head, and took a deep breath.

Time stretched. The dream stranger's face melted into his friend Lucky's haggard visage after Dolly and the babe died. The pain of pity, like a thorny stem being dragged up his throat, went on and on. Then the face melted and took shape as his friend Matthew whose broken ankle kept him behind when his wagon train went on into an ambush and slaughter. Only Matthew blamed himself. The face reshaped again as a despairing soul he had known in the mining camps, then as a dozen others in whom he had sensed a temptation of darkness.

The face blurred into anonymity, and the stranger sprang up from the stool. As he then plunged, the rope snapped taut and the neck broke with a crack that Jack could feel jarring his own bones into wakefulness.

The corpse still hung, beyond help. Jack closed his eyes. He imagined nodding to the corpse and strolling past it to the special map. Those thin filaments glowing red, blue, and yellow stretched from all over the country into the cabin. They joined into a single cable he was following hand over hand down the mountain to the Beckworth Meadows. He gave himself to sleep, less trustingly, but such bliss in the relaxing muscles.

The stranger's face materialized again, but this time the horrible protruding tongue transformed into a huge live snake that came slithering out of the stranger's mouth, its eyes fixed on Jack. Jack could not move as it slithered toward him, slow, sinuous, inexorable. It reared up its head, bared its fangs, and struck. In the split second before it bit, Jack jolted awake. Where had the serpent gone? Gradually the mundane, reassuring cabin came back to him.

There he was again, watching the suicide unfold, but this time the stranger's face was indistinct and Jack's heart was a battleground. He yearned to soothe the stranger off the stool and away from the rope. At the same time he was boiling with rage, wanting to roar at him, "I fought that blizzard beyond what I could do, but you, you just gave up and cast life away?" Did that make his struggle so much trash, the ecstasy up on the pass a mere soap bubble? The rage took hold and he was no longer paralyzed. He brutally forced the stranger's head into the noose. As he kicked the stool away, he felt a spurt of dark joy at the snap of the spine, at the death, at his power.

And then desperate sorrow as he fruitlessly strove to tuck the stool back under the hanged man's feet, as if the hanging could be undone. Did he hate the corpse, hating it for his own revulsion and fear, was that why he had done this hateful murder? As he writhed in self-disgust, he felt the mail shift. This sack, although it weighed so heavy, how could it possibly contain all the love and rage and hope and despair that would sing along those filaments? He conjured the map with the glowing filaments again and stroked the sack. Keeping those filaments alive was up to him. He nestled onto the mail. He was not comforted, but he was surviving.

Suddenly he noticed an almost-silence—just a shiver of breeze in the tips of the pines. The blizzard had moved on, so at least he wouldn't be fighting the wind tomorrow. Sleep took him.

———————◆◆◆◆———————

AT LAST, DAYBREAK pierced the cracks in the walls and door. The sky had cleared, so his journey would be dangerously cold. But here above where eagles soar, every second that the sun shone directly would warm the air. He waited, musing on the mystery of fibers, connecting or killing, till the light shifted pink and gold. He strained to hear the faint susurration of the pine tops. He startled and then smiled as caw followed caw, the jays reviving their raucous conversation. He began to stretch, and every muscle complained.

He opened the door. Brighter and brighter, the sunlight revealed the corpse's eyebrows, reminding him strongly of Lucky, one of his neighbors. How could it be, when he'd never sensed any undertow, any yearning for darkness in the man? Terrible sorrow had afflicted Lucky, but his deep inner strength had pulled him through. He had survived and was building a new life. But Jack felt uncertain, because the face looked alien, so swollen and purple in the morning light. So the light didn't solve the identity problem. But it helped him make some sense beyond the night's horrors. The fat snake the poor man had appeared to be vomiting last night was really just an absurdly large protruding tongue.

Committing every revolting detail to memory so he could faithfully sketch the scene for his friends and neighbors, his gorge stirred, but he forced himself to eat some more pemmican. As he moved about, his aching muscles ached less. Even though the track led downhill from here, each step in the deep fresh drifted powder would devour time and energy. Yet he could feel the gentle, steady pull of the Fort Hotel gathering reeling him toward his goal, toward keeping those bright threads alive. He clung to that. He felt hollow, light-headed. He was going through the motions numbly, but going through them nonetheless. He strapped on his snowshoes. Did the racket dance await?

—Moss Springmeyer grew up on an Angus ranch spanning the Nevada-California border and enjoyed the privilege of taking part in the last cattle drives up to the lush summer ranges at Tahoe. A restless soul, Moss drifted around the world, saddlebags packed with a PhD in statistics. Recently, Moss has settled down with children and grandchildren and has taken to the pen.

INCIDENT ᴬᵀ
THE CIRCLE H

LYNN DOWNEY

JANUARY, 1908
ARIZONA TERRITORY

THE MAN WITH the lantern moved slowly into the muddy tunnel, trying to remember where he'd left the iron box. With memory and luck, he only had to search for a few minutes and there it was, behind the small pile of rocks. He opened it and pulled out a gold bar the size of his hand.

He tossed aside the pick he had used to break through the entrance. It came to rest next to two pale, cracked ironwood supports at the wall to his right. They shimmied with the impact.

A leather saddlebag was draped across his shoulder and he heaved it to the ground. He removed a large canvas holdall and started taking everything out of the box. One, two, three, four... the gold bars were all still here. The small bag of dust was also intact, and so was the larger one full of gold coins. These followed the bullion into the canvas bag.

Intent on his task, the man didn't pay attention to the slight cracking sound beginning to fill the tunnel. But when the noise grew to a
roar he looked up, startled and confused. A rotten timber suddenly
split into kindling, falling toward his head. He bent over, grabbing
the lantern and the canvas bag as an avalanche of rock and dirt began
pouring over him. He straightened and turned to run but was felled
by something sharp which tore into the small of his back.

The lantern flew from his hand in an arc as the man slammed
to the floor. The bag went down with him, scattering the precious
pieces onto the ground next to the light. The last thing he saw before
breath ended and darkness began was a slowly diminishing golden
glow as the bars disappeared under the growing mountain of good
red Arizona soil.

"MAY I SPEAK to you for a moment, Missus Harrison?"

Ellie Harrison stopped walking and turned around to see her
youngest wrangler, Roy Carlson, standing respectfully with his hat
in his hands.

"Sure, Roy, what is it?"

"Well ma'am, it's about the new man, Jesse. Mister Converse,
that is."

"What about him?"

"Well, I don't know if he's up to the work."

"In what way?"

"Well, I just saw him fixing the far gate of the corral and he was,
well, having a hard time. And then he sorta limped back to the barn."

"What are you saying, Roy?"

Carlson caught the tone in her voice and gripped his hat tighter.

"Ma'am, I just think he might be too old for the job."

Ellie smiled slightly. When Jesse Converse had turned up at the ranch three weeks earlier looking for work, Ellie had hesitated at first. He was older than she was, and she was on the wrong side of forty. But he seemed to know his way around a horse, as well as the other livestock. She didn't ask too many questions about his previous jobs. She preferred to judge a man by how he put in a day's work. And if he was a bit creaky, that wasn't a big deal because she was sometimes creaky, too.

Besides, Ellie knew what the real problem was.

She and her late husband Emmett had run the Circle H cattle ranch for twenty years, and after his death three years earlier, she realized she couldn't keep it going on her own, even with the loyal wranglers who'd stuck with her. So, she had turned the Circle H into a dude ranch, which was a new kind of enterprise in Arizona, but she'd heard about some dude outfits that were doing well. It took a while, but she was making a go of things, and a couple of people even came back to the Circle H two years in a row. Ellie knew she had a good location. The town of Wickenburg was far enough away that folks felt they were living out in the desert wilderness, but close enough for her to pick up guests at the train station.

She'd learned quickly that having young, personable cowboys to lead trail rides and chat up the guests was the best way to keep them happy. Especially the "dudines." Roy was one of them, and he liked his dude wrangling work a lot better than his other chores. Anytime Ellie hired a new cowboy, Roy's nose got out of joint, afraid that he'd be knocked off the pedestal he'd built. Not only did he get to flirt with attractive females, they also made sure to give him a nice tip before they left. Ellie thought some of them repaid him for his time in other ways, but nobody had complained yet.

"Are you worried that Jesse will be more popular with the girls than you are?"

The look on his face told her she was right. Jesse might be older than some of the boys by a couple of decades, but he was still handsome—tall, muscular, with piercing blue eyes in a tanned face, his black hair barely silvered. The way he sat on a horse turned heads. But he was indifferent to the dudines, and on his days off she saw him ride into the desert instead of to Wickenburg and its bars, like the younger men.

"Oh, no, ma'am. I just don't want him to get hurt because of his— you know—age."

"Thank you, Roy. I'll keep that in mind."

He'd been dismissed, and he knew it. Roy clapped his hat back on his head and headed for the corral.

Ellie walked into the main lodge where she kept her office. She had built three snug guest cabins around the lodge, which was also the home she had shared with her husband. Her private living quarters and office were in the back of the house, separated from the front parlor, where there was a small reception desk, fireplace, piano, clusters of comfy sofas and chairs, and a phonograph, with a small dining room set into an alcove overlooking distant mountains.

During the day, her guests took trail rides, played badminton, went on desert hikes, or sat in the parlor with its never-empty urn of good coffee and plates of snacks. These were provided by Ellie's cook, Martha, whose daughter Caroline did the housekeeping. Ellie always ate supper with her guests, and before retiring to her own room, she made sure everyone had plenty of playing cards, board games, and records. She also kept a small bookcase filled with novels and books about western history.

The parlor was empty, but it always was in mid-afternoon. She unlocked her office and sat at the desk, gazing at the ledger she'd opened that morning but didn't have the courage to look at again. But it had to be done. Despite a full complement of dudes in this early spring of 1928, she would still be in the red when she closed for the season on May first. She needed new tack and more feed for the growing herd of saddle horses, and had to pay someone to drive all the way from Phoenix to tune the piano. She couldn't scrimp when it came to the guests.

Ellie sighed, closed the ledger, and stood up. She went into her bedroom to get a clean handkerchief and caught sight of herself in the mirror. As usual, her dark blonde hair was falling out of its pins and onto her shoulders. She piled up her hair and absently stuck the pins back in.

She heard the phone ring in her office and walked in to answer it.

"Circle H Ranch, Missus Harrison speaking."

"Hello, Missus Harrison. My name is Bill Gregson. I'm calling to see if you have a cabin available."

"Yes, I do, as a matter of fact. I have one couple checking out today. When would you like to arrive?"

"Tomorrow, if it's convenient."

"Certainly. Will anyone be with you?"

"No, just myself. I'm an anthropologist and a writer. I'm doing some research about the history of the area around the ranch."

"Well, there's plenty to learn, and I have a few books about local history if that will help."

"Yes, that's splendid! I'll arrive around noon tomorrow, if that will suit you."

"Fine, thank you Mister Gregson. How long will you be staying with us?"

"May I keep my departure date open? It all depends on how my research is going."

"Of course, that will be fine. I'll see you tomorrow."

Feeling more optimistic, Ellie made some notes in her registration ledger, and went into the kitchen to check on the dinner menu with Martha.

BILL GREGSON DROVE onto the ranch driveway in a beaten-up roadster exactly at noon the next day. He was around thirty, and looked every bit the absent-minded scholar—horn rim glasses, mussed-up hair, and tweedy clothes. Ellie hoped he'd brought some denims with him, because those khakis would not stand up to long trail rides.

As she checked him in at the desk in the main lodge, she was surprised when he said he would not be participating in any of the dude activities.

"My primary reason for coming here is research, Missus Harrison. This will be my base of operations as I explore the area."

"How much desert exploring have you done?" asked Ellie.

"Quite a bit, actually. I spent a season in some old mines in Nevada, and I am used to long days of hiking. And I understand there are some mining properties around here, too."

"Yes, a lot of gold and silver was found a few miles from here but the shafts were closed up about twenty years ago when they played out. Are you writing a book?"

"Uh…yes, I am thinking about it, depending on what I find."

Ellie finished Gregson's paperwork and handed him a key.

"You are in cabin three, it's just across the way, the furthest one on the left. Do you need any help with your luggage?"

"Not at all, I'll just grab it out of my automobile. May I leave it where it's parked now?"

"Yes. It's unusual for our guests to arrive under their own steam. Your auto looks like it's been in the desert a few times."

Gregson laughed, said it had been, and left the lodge.

Ellie went into her office, leaving the door slightly open. She was poring over the ledger again, surrounded by a pile of bills, when Jesse Converse walked in a few minutes later. Ellie put the papers inside the ledger and closed the cover. A pin fell out of her hair and plinked onto the desk's surface. She made an impatient noise, replaced it, and said, "Yes, Jesse?"

"Missus Harrison, Opal threw a shoe on the morning ride, so I'm going to take care of that, with your permission."

"Of course. You don't need me to tell you what to do."

She had noticed this about him. Everything he did around the ranch he did well, but he never took on a task without checking with her first. Well, maybe that's how things were done at his previous job.

He held his hat in one hand and hesitated for a moment.

"Ma'am, I hope you don't mind me speaking out of turn."

"Go ahead."

"It's just that I wonder if you're having money trouble. Some of the tack is on its last legs, and the tires on your truck are bald. And... well... I hear that you don't eat as much as the guests."

Ellie was astonished, but somehow not angry.

"I don't know where you heard that, but I assure you, I'm well fed. I appreciate your concern, but we'll be fine. I will be replacing the worn-out tack in a couple of weeks."

"I meant no disrespect, Missus Harrison. Just the opposite."

Ellie looked at him and for the first time in years, she got flustered in front of a man. Then she pulled herself together.

"Thank you, Jesse."

He nodded, put on his hat, and left the office.

Ellie let out a long breath. If any other cowboy had talked to her like that, she would have handed him his head and his walking papers. Why did she treat Jesse differently? Surely it wasn't his blue eyes.

Shaking her head, she opened the ledger and went back to work.

After entertaining his fellow guests the next morning with stories of his explorations, Gregson hefted a large rucksack onto his back and headed east. Ellie was relieved to see that he was in jeans, a flannel shirt, and boots. It was still cool, and he had a khaki coat, as well, though he wouldn't need it later. For the next three days, Gregson kept the same schedule, leaving right after breakfast. At his request, Martha made him a packable lunch, and he always returned in time for supper.

One morning, Ellie was behind Gregson as he left the lodge, already shouldering his rucksack. He barreled through the door and crashed right into Jesse, who was coming in. The rucksack fell to the ground, spilling some of its contents—a compass, a notebook, and a rolled piece of heavy paper, which unspooled onto the dirt. Glancing at it, Ellie saw it was a hand-drawn map of some kind. That was interesting, but what caught her attention was Jesse's face.

He had also seen the map and was staring at Gregson with both wonder and a kind of rage. Gregson saw the look, and he blanched and stumbled while he picked up his belongings. He took off, almost at a run, and Jesse watched him until he had disappeared past the rock outcropping beyond the ranch's cabins. Then, without looking at her or saying a word, Jesse walked with purpose toward the bunkhouse.

Over the next two days, Ellie saw Jesse hanging around the corral just before supper, and he watched Gregson as he came back from his rambles. He always saw the cowboy waiting for him, and always looked nervous. Then, Jesse would mount one of the horses and ride into the desert where Gregson had come from. He took longer to return to the ranch each time he went out, which Ellie knew because she asked Roy about it.

"I don't know where he goes, ma'am," he'd said. "I just know that he is more closed-mouthed and stiff than usual when he gets back to the bunkhouse. It was near dark when he strolled in last night."

When Jesse's day off arrived, Ellie got up extra early with a worry she couldn't place. She ate a quick breakfast in the kitchen just after first light, and walked out of the lodge to take in the morning. She was surprised to see Bill Gregson standing there with two saddled horses.

"Oh, good morning, Mister Gregson. Is one of the cowboys taking you on a special ride?"

Gregson looked around before answering.

"No, Missus Harrison. You and I are going riding. How fortunate that you got up so early."

"I'm sorry, I don't have time–"

Before she could finish her sentence, Gregson had pulled a revolver from his rucksack and pointed it at her.

Gesturing to a bay named Goofy, he said, "Get on that horse."

She obeyed, too astonished to speak.

He mounted the other horse, Ginger, pointed east and said to her, "Move."

Turning around to look at Gregson a few moments into their ride she said, "What is this about?"

"Keep your mouth shut and your eyes forward."

Ellie was a skilled rider, and thought about spurring Goofy into a run, but the way Gregson was riding told her he was just as skilled, and had kept this information to himself.

Just as they passed the rocks Ellie sniffed the air.

"Do I smell smoke?"

"Yes. There's a small fire starting in the tack room."

She whipped around again.

"What... why did you do that? You bastard, if any of my guests or animals get hurt, I swear—"

"Oh, please. You're in no position to do anything. Nobody will get hurt, I just needed a distraction."

"What for?"

"I told you to shut up, so shut up."

Feeling sick, Ellie arranged herself in the saddle again. After riding for about three miles, Gregson pointed to another rock and hill formation and told her to ride around to its other side. Then, revolver in hand, he dismounted and told her to get off her horse and walk ahead of him to a nearby pile of lumber and cut-up creosote bush. As she approached it, she saw a large squarish opening in the hill, well over six feet high. Gregson rooted in his pack as he kept his eye on her.

"Walk in," Gregson said. "Take this." He handed her a small flashlight, and he held a much larger one.

"Walk in there? Are you joking?"

"No, I'm not joking, get going."

Taking a deep breath, Ellie walked through the opening.

Her flashlight illuminated carved rock walls with upright, wobbly timbers. She tripped over something and looked down to find a rusted shovel next to a pile of rocks.

"Keep moving." Gregson prodded her roughly with the barrel of the revolver.

After walking a few yards, Ellie noticed that the ceiling seemed to be lower and she worried she might have to start crawling, but then Gregson told her to stop. He shone his light ahead of her and she saw a large circular area full of rotten timber. An old pick was on the ground nearby. Then she saw something else and screamed.

A skeleton.

Gregson told her to go around the debris and stand well beyond it. He then took a small crowbar from his pack and began moving the wood aside. After a few minutes, he reached around the skeleton and grabbed a large canvas bag. It was encrusted with dirt, so stiff it almost crackled. It looked heavy. He dragged the holdall a few feet away from the pile and upturned it.

Six gold bars, shimmering in the glow of his flashlight, fell to the ground. Ellie stared as Gregson picked them up, one by one, and put them in his empty rucksack. He stuck his hand into the crusty bag, pulling out a smaller drawstring satchel, and another that clinked like silver dollars when he tossed it into the pack.

"That doesn't belong to you."

Both Gregson and Ellie looked up sharply and aimed their flashlights in the direction of the voice.

It was Jesse.

Gregson laughed.

"I was sure you'd follow me, though I thought you'd feel it was more important to put out the fire."

"There were plenty of people to put it out. I knew you took Missus Harrison as a hostage in case I followed you. Now you need to let her go."

He pointed a weathered Colt at Gregson, who had also raised his own weapon.

"Just what is this all about?" yelled Ellie. "Is everyone at the ranch all right?"

"Yes, but you lost all your tack, and the shed is gone."

"Goddamit, Gregson," Ellie said. "Why did you do this?"

"Why don't you tell her, Converse?"

Jesse hesitated and then looked at Ellie.

"Missus Harrison, twenty years ago a partner and I robbed a wagon carrying gold bars, dust, and coins from a mine further east, which was on its way to Wickenburg. One of the drivers was badly hurt, but he survived. We stashed the gold here because this shaft had been boarded up. We broke in, hid everything, and then disguised the entrance. We agreed to wait six months before coming back to divvy it up."

"But why is the gold still here, twenty years later?" Ellie asked.

"Because I got caught. I got twenty years at the prison in Florence. I never heard from Bill, my partner, so I assumed he came back and took it all. I also think he turned me in. When I was released, I had to see for myself if the gold was gone, but I couldn't remember exactly where the shaft was."

Jesse looked down at the skeleton.

"I guess he figured I'd never be back for my share, so he decided to take it all. And died trying."

"And you took a job with me so you could find this place." Ellie's face was hard.

"Yes, ma'am. And I'm sorry for that."

He turned to Gregson.

"You're Bill's stepson. He used to talk about you, about what a wrong 'un you were. And you never took his name."

Gregson started to deny it, and then just smiled.

"I found the map under the bedroom floorboards after my mother died a few weeks ago. My stepfather never came back after he left to get the gold, and it broke her heart. She didn't know why he'd gone away, but I did. He told me about the robbery once when he was drunk. I guess he memorized the map and left it behind so he couldn't get ambushed and risk someone else finding the tunnel."

"I recognized the landmarks and Bill's handwriting when you dropped it the other day," Jesse said.

"Huh. I wondered how you knew. Bill never told me his partner's

name. But it wasn't much of a map. I just knew the place was somewhere near the Circle H. So, I kept looking."

"Using my ranch as the base for your research," said Ellie. "You
are foul."

Gregson ignored her, still looking at Jesse.

"And then you started following my tracks every evening, didn't
you? Well, it doesn't matter. Neither of you are getting out of here,
and I'm taking the gold."

"You'll have to kill me first, because if you shoot Ellie, I'll drill you."

Gregson seemed to waver, but he held the gun steady. He cocked
the pistol.

"Ellie, duck!"

Without thought Ellie threw herself to the ground as the tunnel
filled with pistol shots, smoke, and shrieking.

She then heard someone coming toward her, and she grabbed a
sharp piece of wood near her hand. Rolling onto her back she raised
it and then saw Jesse with his hands up.

"It's me, it's me," he said.

She dropped the wood, and he pulled her to her feet. She started
to shake, her hair falling to her shoulders.

"Where is he?"

Jesse pointed to Gregson, writhing on the ground, clutching his leg.

"I didn't kill him, but he'll need a doctor. Are you okay?"

"Yes. Thank you."

She walked up to Gregson and handed him her bandanna. "Here,
put pressure on your leg."

He took it from her and pressed the fabric to the wound, breathing harshly.

Jesse looked at Ellie again as if to make sure she was really all right.
Then he reached for Gregson's pack and slung it over his shoulder.

"I'll leave you one of the horses. Ride to the ranch and get a doctor. Can you find your way?"

"What are you talking about? We're going back together and get him some help. Before I turn him over to the sheriff."

"No, Ellie... Missus Harrison. I'm taking the gold. I'm leaving."

"Oh, I see. Boy, was I wrong about you."

"Prison does things to a man's soul, and mine can't be fixed."

"But the gold isn't yours, any more than it's Gregson's."

"The mine where it came from closed down long ago. There are no owners, no shareholders, nobody can claim it. So, I will."

With a swift movement Ellie leaned over and reached for Gregson's pistol, which he'd dropped on the ground, but Jesse beat her to it. He took a step back, as she sputtered in frustration. He removed the bullets and stuck the empty revolver into the rucksack.

"I know you think you could have shot me. But you wouldn't have. That would not be honorable. You could never be anything else."

He stepped closer to her and for a crazy second Ellie thought he was going to kiss her. But instead, he reached for her hand, held it, and then trotted out of the tunnel.

GREGSON SPENT A few days recovering at the hospital in Wickenburg and was then sent to Phoenix for his kidnapping and attempted murder trial. After a short manhunt, the authorities stopped looking for Jesse Converse, who had disappeared after leaving the two horses at the Wickenburg railroad station. Ellie traveled to Phoenix to testify against Gregson and was more than ready to get back to the peace of the Circle H when the trial was over.

She had worried that people would be scandalized by what had happened and that nobody would want to stay at the ranch, but the opposite happened. Ellie had to turn people down for reservations for the next month. Buying new tack to replace what had burned had taken up most of her savings, but the steady flow of guests ensured an equally steady flow of income. And she was confident she could open again in the fall.

About a week before closing the ranch for the summer, Ellie went into Wickenburg to pick up her mail and do some shopping. The postmistress, Mrs. Smith, said she'd received a package.

Since Ellie usually only got envelopes full of bills, she was intrigued when Mrs. Smith handed her a small parcel, taped solidly shut over butcher paper. The return address was a post office box in a Texas town she'd never heard of. She took it and the rest of her mail and got into her car, which was parked on Center Street. Using a jack knife she kept in the glove compartment, she cut the tape and opened the box.

Inside, surrounded by tissue paper, was a hairpin. A beautiful gold hairpin topped with a luminous pearl. Ellie's jaw dropped as she took it out of the wrapping, and then she saw a small envelope underneath. She ripped it open to find a money order made out to her for $500.

It only took a second to realize who her benefactor was.

It only took five minutes of examining her conscience before she made up her mind.

Ellie put the pin in her hair, the money order in her handbag, and headed for the bank.

—Lynn Downey is an award-winning historian, novelist, and archivist. Her nonfiction books include American Dude Ranch: A Touch of the Cow-

boy and the Thrill of the West *and* Levi Strauss: The Man Who Gave Blue Jeans to the World. *Downey's novel* Dudes Rush In *won a Will Rogers Medallion Award and a New Mexico/Arizona book award. The sequel,* Dude or Die, *was published in 2023. She was the company Historian for Levi Strauss & Co. for 25 years and now works as a consulting archivist. Lynn Downey lives in Sonoma, California and grows wine grapes in her back yard.*

GOLD FEVER

LEE CLINTON

BY THE TIME Billy Lee Taylor had pulled that obstinate mule, Flint, loaded with two hundred pounds of supplies, from Sacramento to Marysville then onto Downieville, much of his enthusiasm for prospecting had gone. It had been a long, tough trip, made worse when searching for a spot amongst those who had already laid claim. The foul-mouthed hostility from men with fire in their eyes and loaded pistols on their belts was downright alarming. One had even fired a shot in his direction while yelling abuse, which forced Billy into unpromising country. On traversing the southern ridges of the Sierras he finally settled on Rock Creek, but what followed just made matters worse.

The constant tedium and hardship, which included the winter of 1851, left him with little to show for his endeavours, just two ounces of gold and a lost year of his youth. His pan and spirits were empty, and the gold fever long gone. It was time to accept failure and return home. This would require giving account to his parents, aunts and uncles, who had financed this venture, all with the expectation that he would make them rich. He could see in his mind's eye the disappointment that would be writ large upon their faces. They had given their blessing by saying, "We'll pray every night for your safe return." It was a nice sentiment, but he knew it implied with full pockets.

It wasn't that the physical endurance was beyond him. Hardship had been no stranger. He'd known tough toils from the sea and on the farm, and he had come across the Oregon Trail as a youngster with his extended family. At twenty-three, he was strong and fit, but it was the loneliness and isolation from family and friends that took its toll. He would dwell on the household routine at the precise time he was thinking of them, and wishing he was there. Finally, the weeks of constant drudgery required to allow luck to intervene for that life changing strike, could no longer be sustained. It was time to surrender.

He had long since sold off Flint, and now it was time to get rid of the rest of his prospecting kit and kaboodle, like the pans, spades, buckets, and sluice box, which were purchased by a neighbouring prospector across in the next gully. The only solace he could muster from his leaving was the fact that he wasn't the first to go. Rock Creek had failed to deliver much to anyone, and many had moved on, leaving only those of unfailing faith or stubbornness to remain. The one item that he kept was his prospecting hammer-pick with its short handle that he tied to his bedroll along with the coffee pot. This was slung over his shoulder along with a calico sack of supplies that included hardtack, salted meat strips, and coffee beans. On his belt was a small leather purse that held his tiny nuggets. He figured it would be enough to get him from Sacramento to the Bay on a barge, then on a berth via a coastal packet north to the Columbia River and back to the Willamette Valley.

What he didn't know was that gold rush prices had continued to increase at an exorbitant rate. The cost of everyday items was excessive unless you had struck it rich. This was going to be a tight budget to get him home. If at all.

THE WALK OUT of the mountains was west to French Corral Creek to pick up the road south to Sacramento. The terrain and vegetation were unhelpful. However, for the first time in a long time, he felt light on his feet. The decision had been made to leave and failure was pushed from his head as his heart filled with the joy of returning home. He walked until the shadows amongst the pines turned to twilight then made camp, setting a small fire for warmth and comfort. Sleep, however, was fitful with dreams of his homecoming being one of disappointment to his family rather than a joyful reunion. Yet, the morning light and a wash in the nearby creek renewed his spirits, and he pressed on.

It was around midday that he stopped to take a break, filling the coffee pot and setting a small fire. When waiting for the water to boil, he looked around at the rocks and pulled out his prospecting pick to split open the shale. It was out of habit and dispensed with once the coffee was brewed. Leaning back on his haunches and feeling the warmth on his hands from the cup, he told himself that he still had a life to live and that was now going to be one of farming.

It was only when lifting his roll back onto his back, as a soft breeze blew up from west, that he caught the disagreeable odour in the air. Some forty yards further down the creek, the smell became pungent, and he expected to find a dead grizzly. But it took another sixty yards before he found the source. Lying face down in the creek was a swollen corpse, heavily blown with maggots. It was a fellow prospector, his tools of trade close by. Billy approached the body tentatively and with a stick, tried to lift the head to see the face. In doing so, the bloated skin at the back of neck split open to spill a mass of squirming larvae that let forth a fierce rotten stink. He dropped the stick and turned his head, gagging, before spitting out the bitter taste of coffee retched up from his stomach.

Moving a little further upwind, he was able to turn back and look upon the wretched sight, but in doing so, he still needed to press his nose into the crook of his arm. To stay and bury the poor unfortunate soul was beyond his means. He consoled this lack of decency by not having the tools available. Yet, protruding from under the body was the handle of a shovel. As a substitution, he removed his hat and offered a silent prayer of condolence and finished with the words, "Rest in peace."

It was only by chance that his eye caught the view of the shanty, higher up on the ridge where it was hidden amongst the firs. He made his way up the steep embankment with the intention of finding a name that he could then report to the authorities in Sacramento. An act of decency and a small sign of duty and respect. Little did he know that this minor detour would change the circumstances of his life forever.

Inside the small dim cabin, that burrowed back into the ridge, was a wooden cot with a hessian palliasse. Some shelves, made from packing boxes, held a few dry goods, and to one side of the door was a small bench with a three-legged stool. Some kitchen utensils sat upright in a tin cup that rested upon an upturned tin plate. This was a man of discipline who kept his shelter shipshape. A book lay next to the oil lamp on the shelf by the bed. Billy picked it up and opened the worn cover looking for a name, there was none, just the initials of J.E. and below Class IV in faded ink. Titled Geography Made Easy, he paused at a map of the Pacific Northwest, running a finger down the coast over the names of Dixons Entrance, Charlottes Bay, Cape Gregory, and Albion. A coast he knew well when he served before the mast on the coastal trade in his teens. Had he not returned home after the death of his older brother, when crushed by a falling tree, he would still be at sea and now senior enough to take on the responsibilities of a third or even second mate. At the very back of the book in light pencil was a list of numbers in two columns. These had been written by turning the book from head to toe. To view these, he had to leave the cabin and allow the sunlight to brighten the pencil entries. Billy was unable to decipher their meaning and after a final look around the cabin, he placed the school atlas back beside the lamp and left.

He had travelled less than a quarter of a mile before it started to dawn on him what the numbers may have meant. Had the first column been dates and the second a list of measures in ounces of weight? And if so, was it a tally of the dead prospector's gold findings? He tried to remember the figures and add them up in his head. But what he came up with couldn't be right, as it was more than ninety. With gold fetching around seventeen dollars an ounce that would be worth $1,500. He paused and looked back up the creek in the direction of the shack. Should he go back and check, or move on and leave the dead to their secrets?

Billy re-entered the dim cabin and took the book back out into the sunlight to sit upon a stump and re-read the jottings. He was wrong, the numbers he remembered were well short of the final total. They added up to 143, or if his hunch was right, a payout close to $2,500. The question that now swirled in his head was, could this be true? And if so, where was the gold? He stepped back into the cabin and stood looking for a hiding place, examining each inch before beginning a detailed physical search. He looked under the bed, under the small table, turning the stool upside down, removing the dry goods from the shelf, and even pressed his cheek to the rough wall to see if it hid a secret recess. He stamped upon the earth floor seeking to hear any hollow sound, but nothing was revealed. He walked around the outside of the cabin to where the walls had been dug back into the ridge, but once again he found nothing. A small track at the back led further up over the ridge to a pit with a straining post. On turning back from the privy to return to the cabin he saw a flat rock jutting from the embankment at waist height. It looked out of place. Below this little platform were scuffed boot prints. It looked like a little bench, but for what purpose? Billy pulled at the adjoining rocks and felt one move. He eased it back, and there hidden in a crevice were two cloth bags. The first, with the embroidered initials J.E. which held a small wooden box containing scales and weights. Tucked in behind that was a heavier bag, weighing about nine or ten pounds. He knew immediately what it was with its loose contents. This was the prospector's haul. He pulled open the draw string to glance inside just as the sunlight flashed through the overhead branches and upon the gold nuggets within. The sight took his breath away. What he was looking at was a fortune beyond belief. It was mesmerising, as if the gods had chosen to bestow upon him an ethereal gift.

They hadn't.

It was something else. One deeply entwined within the frailty of man's nature. He had just been struck with gold fever.

———————◆◆◆◆———————

THE TREK OUT of the mountains gave Billy time to think. He had left a dead man unburied and taken his winnings. These were sobering and uncomfortable thoughts for a young man, who now began to push them aside by telling himself that firstly he had broken no laws, well at least none that he could think of. The prospector had died suddenly, just like neighbour Lucas Beam had done when they found his body in the field lying in a furrow behind his mule. Therefore, the prospector's time was up. Nature had taken its course. Secondly, the treasure had been found through his thoughtful observations and deductions. It was, he tried to convince himself, as if a hand had guided him, and besides, he had only sought to find the identity of the prospector not his gold. If he had not found the body, then surely someone else would have done so. Although he had to concede, maybe not the gold, so therefore maybe it was divine intervention after all. If not for him, the hiding place may never have been found, doing no good for anyone, and good was how Billy planned to share his bonanza with family and friends to make their lives secure and agreeable. Was this not the very reason why he had come to California? All these deductions made so much sense that all previous concerns now just disappeared.

It was of course an exercise in self-delusion, laced with excuses and half-truths to sidestep and accommodate that moral dilemma that befalls all those who seek to avoid what is as clear as the nose on their face. Billy Lee Taylor had stolen from the dead. If his intentions were virtuous, he would have considered how he was going to tell his father of the true circumstances of his prize. But that thought never crossed his mind. He had now convinced himself that he had paid his dues as a prospector and that the sack of gold had been earnt by his own good efforts and luck, and luck was what every prospector depended on.

On arriving in Sacramento, he cashed in five ounces of gold with Schliemann & Co, receiving $86.25. It seemed like a small fortune but on paying for a bath, shave, and the purchase of a river ticket, all at excessive prices, only half remained. His desire for new clothes would have to wait until he got to San Francisco.

⎯⎯⎯⎯⎯◆⎯⎯⎯⎯⎯

THE HUSTLE AND bustle on the city streets were more than a little unnerving for Billy, who was unaccustomed to crowds that bumped and jostled without a by your leave. He clutched the gold to his chest inside his coat and eyed each face with suspicion. His distrust increased when he ventured into Chinatown giving second thoughts to his plan not to trade via an agent or private bank. To do so would require the signing of papers. Chinamen asked no questions.

The chalkboard street sign said gold dust and nuggets traded. He entered to the smell of burning incense and pulled the bag from under his coat. At the table an elderly Chinaman spread out a black cloth and waved a hand back and forth. Billy emptied the contents, and each smooth nugget was sorted in size and viewed through an eyeglass under the light of a mirror oil lamp. The largest nugget, of some three fingers in width, was scraped. Billy knew there was no need to test for impurities. All had come from the river, washed smooth by time and of pure gold. Each was then weighed and recorded in a ledger. The final count was, as the dead prospector had accounted, 143 ounces. A slip of paper was written upon and pushed before Billy with an exchange rate of $15.43 per ounce. Billy knew he could get $18 with a little shopping around and that the Chinaman, as a trader, would get more than $20 on-selling. But this was a cost he would have to bear. Right now he needed a transaction without questions. The exchange calculation was made on an abacus and came to $2,206.49 and was offered via a variety of foreign coins. He shook his head. He wanted US currency.

"It will cost you more," said the Chinaman.

"How much more?" asked Billy.

The beads on the abacus flicked to each end and the new calculation shaved off $200. He was undecided, until he saw the glint and heard the clink of the twenty dollar liberty heads as they cascaded upon the counting cloth. It was a king's ransom, and he nodded his agreement. For five dollars he was offered a canvas money belt with a strap buckle and a small purse fitted to the front to hold cash for immediate use. When loaded up it weighed just over seven pounds, yet when fitted it didn't restrict movement and was well hidden under his shirt. The deal was now done. All he had to do now was get back home safely.

At Portsmouth Square he purchased a flannel shirt for $2.50, trousers for $4.50, and new boots for $6.00. While sitting in the changing booth, he placed two of the gold coins under the innersole of each boot, a practice he had used in his seafaring days, but never with a coin worth $20. His final purchase was a carpet bag to hold his old clothes and prospecting pick. It would be the one item he would keep, to remind him of his time in the California goldfields.

When it came for the purchase of a ticket home, it was more difficult than he expected. The docks were in chaos and while the harbour was full of ships, nearly all had been abandoned by their crews who had left for the goldfields. He was told that he would need to return daily and walk the docks in search of a packet heading north from the few still vying their trade up and down the coast. This now meant finding a place to stay. He was pointed toward Alta Street, where, on passing a saloon on Union Street a sign offered comfort to the weary traveller. He told himself that it would allow him to ask about board until he got a berth. In theory, the short detour sounded fine. In practice it was folly. The sign also said, Girls Within. As he went to cross the threshold an elderly dishevelled man advised, "You be careful, laddie, there be vipers in there."

Billy dismissed the warning. The last thing he needed was to be cautioned by a rambling old evangelist. Or so he thought.

LONELY NIGHTS IN the mountains had primed Billy's desire for feminine charm that now presented itself in the form of a redhead going by the name of Ruby. She was younger by a couple of years, but experienced in the ways of the world of which Billy was blissfully ignorant.

Her opening line of, "Hello stranger, what brings you to San Francisco?" had been used a thousand times by dozens of Rubies, Jades, and Sapphires, just to name but a few who traded on a gemstone moniker, yet this unsolicited introduction sparkled fresh in Billy's ears. When she leaned in close, he could smell the scent of lavender.

"Would you like to buy me a drink?" she asked.

"Sure, I don't drink myself, but..."

She cut him short. "Whiskey and a special, thanks Tyrone."

Billy went to protest.

"You need to buy a drink for me and one for yourself, if you want my company."

"Okay, I guess," was his uncertain response as he presented a gold coin.

Billy watched as Tyrone the barman poured two small glasses, one of a dark liquid and other almost clear. The change he received in return was ten dollars. The cost of the two drinks at five dollars each seemed ridiculously overpriced.

However, his deliberations on profligacy were disturbed when Ruby clicked his glass and announced. "Drink up."

On putting it to his lips, he could smell molasses, while the taste was of smoky wood. It burnt as he swallowed, to be followed by a warm glow. This was not surprising as it was 120-proof. He looked over at Ruby's drink. "What's that?" he asked. "Must be very special." The inference being on the price.

It was lemon water, but Ruby had a different explanation as she leaned in close, their cheeks almost touching as she whispered. "The drink pays for getting to know me."

"Oh," said Billy, "is that how it works?"

"That's how it works. When you order me a special, then I'm here just for you." Billy went to question, but Ruby put a finger to his lips. "Think of it as an investment and in return you get my undivided attention, almost."

He thought for a moment. "Almost?"

"This bar is rather public, and a lady has to be careful of her reputation when talking to a stranger."

Billy nodded vigorously in agreement as he took a step back.

Ruby moved forward to fill the space. "But we could hide away, should you care to purchase a booth."

Billy looked around for the booths.

She pointed an upright finger. "On the mezzanine."

He glanced up to see a wall of red velvet curtains. Without thinking he said, "Looks expensive."

"Ten dollars for each half hour. But why don't we put an hour to one side just to get to know each other."

Billy, like all young country men, had been warned about city saloon gals and their ways, but the close presence of one who wanted to get to know him was a whole new experience. By now his glass was empty and the fire of the alcohol matched her redheaded beauty. In fact, it made the proposal seem like a good deal, which just goes to show how muddled headed a man can be at times. Had he paused to think, he would have recalled that the cost of the new plow that his father had purchased less than two years ago was under ten dollars. Friends and neighbours had come from afar to admire the contraption. Was an hour with Ruby worth two brand new John Deere polished steel shovel plows?

SEDUCTION IN A gold rush doesn't come cheap. Billy Lee Taylor spent well over one hundred dollars getting to know Ruby that mostly consisted of glasses of lemon water and shots of whiskey. The conversation was sparse, replaced mostly by heavy breathing. To say that he had fallen under Ruby's spell was akin to stating that a rising flood can cause wet feet. So, when she suggested that they meet around the back, near the livery stable, as she was about to get off work, it seemed to him to be a capital idea. That his legs were a little wobbly when ascending the back stairs of her boarding house, ought to have given fair warning that he may not have been up to the task he had in mind. However, by then it was all too late for our love-struck Romeo.

What exactly transpired thereafter was a mystery, as he was unable to remember, when awoken by loud banging upon the door. He looked around. Ruby had gone and so had his trousers, along with his money belt. He had been fleeced.

On opening the door, a grim rotund man who looked a lot like the barman at the saloon, demanded payment for the room. Billy shook his head and tried to focus, advising that Ruby wasn't home, and he should come back later if rent was overdue.

"You used the room. You settle up," was the response.

Billy, clutching bedclothes around his waist, started to stammer.

The man cut him short. "I'll get you a pair of trousers."

Billy felt both relieved and grateful.

"It will be fifty for the room and twenty for the trousers. Seventy in all. The maid will be up in a minute. Give her the cash."

He went to protest as the door slammed shut in his face.

Billy stumbled backwards to drop down onto the side of the bed. What followed was humiliation, guilt, and remorse. It took an age before he could muster the presence of mind to search the room in the forlorn hope of finding his money, all the time asking himself, how could Ruby have done such a thing? He found nothing, no money, and no sign of Ruby. The finalisation of the bill was only possible from the eighty dollars he had placed in his boots, now leaving him with just ten dollars to get home.

He quizzed the maid on the whereabouts of Ruby who said she didn't know anyone by that name, but she also failed to make eye contact. Billy smelt a rat. He asked about the man who had demanded payment and if he worked at the saloon. Once again, the maid was evasive, but this time she also showed fear.

***

WHEN RICHES ARE taken from a man, he's bound to get angry and seek redress. But when you take from him his dignity, leaving him with no self-respect, he tends to get dangerous. It is as if he has nothing of value left to lose. Billy entered the saloon with determination, looking for Ruby and Tyrone the barman. He found neither before being escorted from the premises by force. He stood in the dust on the street and felt like a dog who had just been kicked.

"Been taken for a ride, laddie?"

Billy turned to see the evangelist who had offered advice when entering the saloon the previous day. "Yeah, by a barman named Tyrone and a girl named Ruby," he bitterly lamented.

"Tar and roses."

Billy had no idea what he was talking about.

"The rose is sweet, but she's tarred by the brute. And if I was to tell you where you might find them, you may be in more trouble than you are in now."

"On that I'll take my chances."

"You armed then? You need to be armed."

Billy had never carried a sidearm, and he wasn't going to start now. He just wanted his money back, and if he had to split the difference, then something was better than nothing, even if it was fifty-fifty. "You know where I'll find them?"

The man nodded. "Cost you."

"How much?"

"Ten."

Billy bit on his lip and looked around, contemplating. "Take me to them, then I'll pay you."

"I don't like getting too close to Tyrone. If he found out I'd put the finger on him, he'd kill me." The look of fear on the old man's face was genuine. "I'll show you where you can find the girl. Tyrone will be close by, but I ain't going in. No sir."

Billy knew he was being squeezed, but what choice did he have. "Okay," he said.

———————✦———————

THE THREE-STORY timber framed building was behind the saloon and adjacent to the boarding house.

The old man pointed up a steep flight of stairs at the back. "Up there. Doors latched, but the key is hidden under the railing. But I wouldn't go in there unarmed. You don't seem much of a match for Tyrone."

"I don't want a fight, I just want to talk, that's all, and get back what was taken."

"Tyrone is not the talking kind." The old man was agitated. "Give me my money now."

Billy passed across his last coin.

When he got to the landing, he tried to open the door. It was latched. He ran his hand under the railing and couldn't find the key. Had he been duped again? He looked back down, but the old man was gone. Squatting, he looked under the railing and there in a recess was the key held in place by a magnet. He opened the door to the sound of the latch and voices coming from down a dim corridor. As he advanced it became clear that an argument was in progress, but the words were muffled. He stopped outside the door, unsure as to what to do next, when he heard a scream and a thump of a body hard upon the floor. He turned on the handle and eased it open. The words were now clear.

"Give me all of the money, or I swear I'll kill you."

"I've given it to you already, that's all there was, a hundred dollars."

"I know you're lying. You've done this before, keeping money for yourself and trying to run off. Where is it?"

Billy eased open the door a little further to view Tyrone, knife in hand, standing over Ruby.

"You want to be cut? You want your pretty face scarred for life?"

Ruby lay on the floor in tears. Her arm up to defend herself.

Billy placed the carpetbag down quietly, opened the bag's latch and withdrew his prospecting pick, tightening his grip around the handle and lifting it high. He then pushed the door fully open.

Tyrone turned to see Billy's silhouette in the doorway.

"Run Billy," shouted Ruby. "He'll kill you."

Tyrone hurled himself forward, extending his arm as the silver blade flashed.

Without a moment's thought Billy swung the pick down, the point entering the skull near the left temple to the sickening sound of cracking bone and squelching brain. The big man's eyes rolled back as dark red blood gushed from the fatal wound. Billy pulled the pick from the skull and the body slumped to the floor, the left leg violently kicking as urine puddled between the legs.

Ruby kept her eyes on Tyrone as she addressed Billy, "I think we need to get out of here."

THE HOMECOMING WAS a joyous event mixed with sheer relief for Billy Lee Taylor. On the front porch he hugged his mother tight.

"Back safe and sound," she said. "You were always in our prayers and the good Lord delivered."

"Were you lucky?" asked his father. "Did you strike it rich?"

"I sure did, Father," said Billy lifting the money belt high above his head. "And that's not the only treasure I brought back from California. Mom, Dad, I'd like to introduce you to my new wife, Missus Ruby Taylor."

—The author is an Australian writer of ten Western novels published under the pen name of Lee Clinton in the Black Horse Western (BHW) series. Unfortunately, the UK publishing house responsible for the BHW series has now discontinued that line of books, however, the author's novels remain available worldwide in digital form via Amazon. In the meantime, he has now turned his hand to short stories as he continues his love of the American Western. Lee is based in Western Australia, the largest of the Australian states, where he is now retired after a career in the military. His Western titles include Raking Hell, The Mexican, Coyote, *and* Animal Instinct.

ON THE LASSEN TRAIL

JOHN BLANCHARD

PICKING UP A brand from the fire, Krup walked around to Daskin and held it threateningly in his face.

"You," shouted Krup. "I have listened to *you* long enough."

For an instant, the flame lit up Daskin's haggard face, bearded and hollow-eyed.

"*Git* that away from me," he said, swatting the torch with his hand.

From out on Goose Lake came the weird yodeling of a loon.

Krup staggered back and fell heavily on a crate, breaking it.

"Oh, oh," he cried, in his German accent. "Why did I efer listen to you? Ohhh...."

"You make me sick," said Daskin, spitting.

Getting up heavily, Daskin staggered over to a decrepit wagon, ripped a splintered board from its bed, and threw it on the fire. Picking up his bottle of whiskey, he took a long pull on it and listened. For an instant, he sensed, more than he heard, the still dark presence of myriad waterfowl. For no reason at all, except that their peacefulness disturbed him, he shouldered his double-barreled shotgun and fired in their direction. At once the birds began a rippling chorus of throaty squabbling. As the noise echoed back from the mountains on the other side of the lake, an invisible spume of fowl rose in a tumultuous wave, composed of thousands of beating wings, and settled again on the water.

Daskin swore he could feel the wing beats from where he stood. "Damn," he said. "Missed...."

It was disquieting, though. Something had gone very wrong. He didn't belong where he was. Something else had possession of the place and didn't want him there. But there he sat, day after day, guarding his liquor, as if it meant more to him than all the gold in California. His head ached fearsomely. Nevertheless, he tried to bring it round to some conception of the last six months. Yes, something had gone wrong. He had stopped writing in his diary—that was one thing. There had been something right about that. It was something to do every day—clean and wholesome... and sane. Although he had stopped writing, he still ticked off the facts in his head—*"Commences cloudy, light northerly breeze, temperature fifty degrees. Breakfasted on boiled ox and whiskey...."* Every day, unfailingly, he had written—no matter how he ached, no matter how his eyelids drooped at night, or how hard the dust flew in his face at midday. He had made his entry nonetheless. Maybe no one would ever read it. No matter, he knew he had his reasons, though what they were precisely he could not have said. Now, he seemed to understand, and it frightened him. That simple, dull, repetitive, aggravating habit had kept mind and soul together, just as meat had kept body and soul together.

When had he given it up?

Daskin leaned his gun against a tree and grabbed another brand from the fire. Holding it aloft, he climbed inside the wagon where he kept his belongings and hauled out a leather satchel. With his free hand he clumsily undid the ties and began rummaging inside, spilling things on the ground. His head spun, his eyeballs ached, and his hands trembled—symptoms of disintegration. *I need a drink,* he thought. He let the pack fall to the ground. He couldn't remember.

When they had come to the forks....

He was still writing then. Both roads were broad and beaten. At the "post office"— an old whiskey barrel with a hole cut in the top— he'd found letters from those who had gone before— people he knew. How could so many people have been wrong? But mile stretched into mile— animals died, people died, and still the destination stretched ahead, ever farther ahead.

When had he stopped writing?

Daskin returned to the fire. Alcohol kept a chill off temporarily, but then froze you. He threw more boards on the fire and sat down against a fallen tree. The flames licked skyward. The heat radiated toward him. Krup lay next to the broken crate, moaning. In the light, Daskin saw his boyish face, his upturned nose, and the pout on his lips. His face was swollen, his lower lip distended. Somehow, he did not feel anything when he looked at him—no compassion, no sorrow. Nothing.

In a single draught, he drained his whiskey bottle.

"Oh, what a fool I was," Krup wailed.

Daskin had noticed a certain coldness in himself, much as the weather had turned cold. Death was simply a fact he took note of. He ticked off the deaths, as he ticked off the facts of meteorology, or as he counted the dead oxen beside the trail—the abandoned wagons and personal belongings. Once he had felt something even for the lowly oxen. It had pained him to see them suffer, to see how they bellowed for water, became weak for lack of forage. Dumb beasts that they were, they pulled the wagons till they dropped.

He stayed drunk. But when the alcohol wore off....

He didn't like to think what he felt.

Pahute Peak, for example. It lay along the trail, not long after the forks, if he remembered correctly. He'd had a sickening feeling. The emigrants had agonized about the decision so much, there were bound to be misgivings when they had gone so far along the chosen fork that turning back was out of the question.

How was it possible that no one really knew for sure which way was best? They had trusted, thinking that no matter which way they went, the remainder of the journey was but a small fraction of the distance they had already traversed.

Many months earlier, having just left the settlements, the gold seekers hadn't worried much when mountains and buttes and strange far-off shapes loomed up alongside the trail, because they knew that ranches and army outposts, however meager, still lay ahead—places where they could still mail a letter, buy a meal, or get a wagon repaired. The odd scenery conjured images in the mind, but for the most part, they associated them with thoughts of home.

Beyond the forks, it was a different story. By now, they hadn't seen a human settlement in hundreds of miles, and the only other people they saw were Indians.

Then Pahute Peak loomed up. In the brilliant, crystalline air of the desert, the snowcap gleamed blindingly. Yet no water whatsoever streamed from it into the parched arroyos at its base.

Somehow, all the romance had gone out of the scenery. Daskin thought he was looking at mountains and deserts for the first time. His mind no longer conjured up images of castles and battlements and airy seats of mythological beings. Now, he felt that what surrounded him was something wholly other than himself, something he could no longer measure or compare with any standard he was familiar with.

He realized that what he saw, what shouldered right next to him along the trail, was something completely inhuman, something completely indifferent to his well-being.

Around that time he had stopped writing, and he had stopped precisely because he had no longer known what to say. He had started drinking more, instead. But he hadn't noticed till now, that the less he wrote and the more he drank, the more he had come to feel just like his surroundings—alternately huge and cold and impassive, like the peaks, or featureless, salt-encrusted and flat like Black Rock Desert, or hard and sharp like columns of tufa. He could almost expand himself, project or lie flat or crust up. He might burn himself or cut his foot and feel nothing. He was a part of it all.

Krup's persistent whine brought him back to the present.

"I trusted you," he said. "Now we are the last ones."

The last ones, thought Daskin. He hadn't really thought about it. The emigrant party had completely disintegrated, leaving only him and Krup. Perhaps they really were the last ones.

Krup turned over on his side and was quiet for a while. He began to make a strange whimpering noise. Occasionally he sobbed loudly. Two months earlier, that sound would have gone through Daskin like a knife. But now, he only took note of it, as if it were the racketing of a woodpecker. The only feeling he had anymore was rage.

After a while, Krup fell asleep and began snoring.

In the firelight, Daskin's face was a twisted and haggard mask—a pasteboard which squinted and frowned and twitched in one cheek. The more he concentrated, the more he furrowed his brow and stared like a madman....

Precisely when had the emigrant party begun to disintegrate?

This question—impossible to answer with any degree of precision—now began to occupy Daskin as he reclined against his log.

While he thought, the night wind ripped at the flames and blew a shower of sparks vertically across the ground.

When, precisely? Was it before the forks, or after? Surely it had been before. In a traveling party so loose-knit and poorly organized, signs of strain and fracture were bound to start showing up right away. Other parties he had seen were better prepared. The men wore military-style uniforms, governed themselves with a constitution and a set of by-laws. They had begun planning months in advance and were therefore well-provisioned and organized. His own party was of another type. They had caught the gold fever late and set out at the last minute, when the season was almost too far advanced. Earlier travelers had used up all the fuel. Their livestock had consumed the grass. His own party had started to fall apart well before the forks. It had never been an organized emigrant party in the first place. Mustn't a group integrate, become close-knit, before it can disintegrate? If a collection of marbles starts to roll around on a table and falls all over the floor, isn't that because it's nothing but a collection of marbles?

Daskin shook his head. What did marbles have to do with anything? In any case, the signs of decay were there from the start. Guard duty dereliction was always one of the first signs. After a hard day on the trail—breaking camp, harnessing teams, eating trail dust and fording rivers, making camp again at night—after that, nobody wanted to stay up and stand guard. Everybody wanted to sleep. Yet the ability to maintain that simple system of discipline and routine made all the difference. In his own party, the system broke down almost immediately.

It seemed like a century ago.

WHEN DASKIN AWOKE in the morning, he could see only a faint reddish glow in the east. It was still very early. He couldn't remember when or how he had fallen asleep—or if he had really slept at all. As often happened on this interminable journey, his first sensation upon waking was one of bewilderment. He couldn't remember where he was. Cruelly, for a few moments he imagined he was still at home, or farther back on the trail in happier times. When he finally remembered, the anguish and bitterness he felt were almost unendurable. At one time, he would have included a summary of his feelings among the morning's notations in his notebook—a kind of weather report on his soul—at times stormy and roiled like the surface of a northern sea, at times brilliant with sunlight, agitated with sorrow, or on fire with anger. As long as he recorded each mutation he was free to move on to the rest.

Now, however, his first act upon waking was to take a long pull from a fresh whiskey bottle.

When the liquor had sufficiently deadened his horror so that he could move, Daskin sat up stiffly and supported himself against the log behind him. He had evidently fallen asleep where he lay. The fire had long since died. The air was sharp and frosty, and he was shaking with cold. Evidently, he had remembered to cover himself with a blanket, or he might be dead. Krup, too, lay under a blanket in the same place as before, his head completely covered. The nighttime sky had been awash with starlight, but in the pale light of dawn, the sky was now an unbroken sheet of gray.

Commences cloudy, thought Daskin, automatically. *Wind north-north-east. Temperature—?*

In order to record the temperature, he would have to get out his instruments. For a moment he thought fondly of his instruments. They were among the things he still carried with him, along with his journals, his shotgun, and several bottles of whiskey. Now that the last animals had died, these meager belongings would be difficult to carry.

The temperature had certainly fallen. A layer of rime encrusted the blankets like tufa. The land creeps over a man at night as he lies insensible and begins to claim his body for its own. So what if it seeks to destroy your soul? Perhaps it knows how useless that organ has become. Perhaps it only seeks to free us from our sufferings, to transmute us into dry lake beds and volcanic badlands, so that we, too, might become impassive observers.

Daskin thought about getting up and finding his thermometer and notebooks. First he would have to start a fire, begin the whole laborious process of making the morning camp. But he was too demoralized. And because he was demoralized, so was Krup. Krup had depended on him. As the older man, Daskin had made all the key decisions. He had become the father that Krup had left behind in Germany—a man who had never been much of a father anyway, it seemed. Krup didn't like to talk about him. He wouldn't say anything at all about the old country, except inadvertently. These random remarks, however, had given Daskin the impression of an embittered young man, but a man who was still very inexperienced and naive, foolish enough— as Krup now realized—to have attached himself wholeheartedly to a man more embittered than himself. You couldn't really blame him. The bitterness in his mentor had not really begun to show up till after the forks. Even at that point, Daskin was still recording every mile of the journey in his books and was still confidently and soberly deliberating every decision. Nor could you blame Daskin. He had fallen victim to the same misinformation that had deceived hundreds of others.

Peter Lassen's scheme to do a profitable trade with the emigrants when they arrived at his *rancho* in California.

Perhaps the bitterest pill, thought Daskin, as he lay against his log, drinking his whiskey, was this loss of confidence, not only of Krup's, but of his own in himself. Yes, he had needed Krup as much as Krup needed him. That was why, as everything else fell apart around them, they alone had stayed together. The bond which had formed between them, of slight duration but cemented through hardships, was almost as strong as blood.

But no longer. Krup had finally realized that Daskin was no stronger, no smarter, nor any better than most men. When the hardships had piled up after the forks, Daskin had crumbled like anyone else. He had started drinking, at first getting drunk at night only, then earlier and earlier every day, until he was almost too drunk in the morning to break camp. Pretty soon he had stopped writing altogether, and after that he began neglecting almost every necessary detail of trail life, leaving it all to Krup. On top of that, he had become very abusive.

"Temperature?" At least twenty degrees colder. Twenty degrees in one night. And that sky. It could only mean one thing. Was the season so far advanced that a big storm was already on the way? Daskin shuddered, as he had shuddered a hundred times before. But this time it had a different quality. It began on the outside with the chill, just as it always did when the fire died down, and the whiskey wore off. But now it went inside and began shaking him there, shaking him to the core, until he thought that something must be coming loose inside, like a man losing his grip on a life raft.

Daskin forced himself to his feet, staggered a few steps until he regained his balance. I've stayed here too long, he thought with alarm. What the hell was I thinking?

Krup still lay motionless on the ground. Down by the lake, the waterfowl were beginning to stir as the shadow of the mountains lifted from the still surface of the water. A breeze came up and whistled through the pine trees.

Daskin began feverishly rummaging through his things in the ruined wagon bed.

No time to get warmed up, he thought. *No time to eat. Got to get a move on. Walking'll warm me up. Sun's not even up yet. Should be able to make thirty miles before night fall. That should put me in striking distance of the ranchos in the valley.*

Daskin's eyes glowed like two embers in a dying fire. He was kidding himself. He really had no idea how far he was from the settlements. He ripped and tore at the bundles and sacks in the wagon bed, cursing under his breath. Working feverishly, he made up a small pack, containing his instruments, notebooks, and a couple bottles of whiskey. He tucked a knife in his belt, rolled up his blanket and tied it to his pack, and shouldered his double-barreled shotgun.

Then he reentered the trail and began rapidly walking.

Daskin knew now that he and Krup were two of the last few people to come straggling along the trail at the very last possible moment that season. No one else had come down the trail past the camp where he and Krup had malingered. That had never happened before, whenever they had stopped to rest.

This fact now began to occupy his thoughts as he hurried along. He tried to pace himself, but at every step he found himself struggling to control his rising anxiety. He was still in middle-age. But even so, he didn't have quite the vigor of his youth, and the hardships of the trail, plus weeks of whiskey drinking, had worn him down.

"Wind shifting, coming south. Temperature still dropping. Trail littered with debris, broken wagons, discarded harness, piles of clothes, sheet-iron stoves, dead oxen."

A creek descended out of the lake. The trail followed it down through a rocky defile and into a high grassy valley. Daskin soon fell into the familiar rhythm of walking as the storm seemed to hold off, and the temperature became steadier. The wind began to blow erratically, now from one quarter, now from another, finding every chink in his clothing, chilling him to the bone.

"Meridian cloudy, wind shifting constantly. Trail moves in a southerly direction. Forgot to pack food... pack too heavy... may have to discard some things."

Having abandoned Krup—yes, that was the only word to describe it—Daskin suddenly realized that for the first time during the entire journey, he was completely alone. Illogically, he began to laugh, and the sound that came out of him was loud and frantic and cackling, like a tree full of crows. But was it any more illogical to laugh than it was to have abandoned his only companionship? He began to wonder if he had not abandoned Krup, not for the reason he supposed—that he had panicked—but rather because he had wanted to be alone. And the part of him that had wanted this solitude was not the small everyday part of him that carped and debated and planned. No. It was some part of him that lay hidden from sight, a being with a personality all its own, whose existence within him he had heretofore barely suspected. This being, he now realized, had schemes and desires and plans which did not coincide with his and which he couldn't fathom. Why on earth had he left Krup lying there by the trail? What advantage was there in setting off by himself, depriving himself of the society and assistance of a younger able-bodied man?

Rubbish! He thought. *Ain't no such thing. Who was putting such rubbish in his head? Funny thing, what a man begins thinking....*

When Daskin stopped for the day, he had just enough energy to make a small fire, spread his blankets, and lie down upon them in exhaustion. When he closed his eyes, he saw a sheet of blank paper. Soon the words began to come, automatically, looking for some resting place.

"Sunset cloudy and calm. Wind south-east. Made twenty-five miles to-day. Camped on ridge of spur that heads south-west from prominent snow butte that has been visible to the east all day. Food scarce. Most carcasses far gone. Very hungry after so much exercise.... Thoughts chaotic. Nerves jumpy. There's a demon that's been following me all day, I'd swear it. Caught a glimpse of the devil once or twice. Just enough to quicken my pace.... What bitter thoughts—loneliness, sorrow—assail a man in this wilderness—black thoughts that don't bear examination, but become all the more insistent for all that. I think of my journal, but the thought of taking up my pen produces a violent revulsion. It strangles within me. My hand is crabbed with disuse, with clutching at whiskey bottles, and all my words are air, nothing but smoke from countless camp fires, unrecorded....

"Nov—Commences with light freezing rain and snow. Wind blustery from the south. Breakfasted on putrid ox meat, flour boiled in water, and the usual whiskey. Running out of everything, if I ever had it. What I wouldn't give for a cup of strong coffee with a little sugar in it. Hated to leave the fire, but I have no shelter here and must get somewhere safe, if not to the ranch then at least fall in with someone ahead, if any are still on the trail...."

How long was it since he'd left Krup? Was it five days or was it two? Daskin knew he must be getting near the Great Valley, which he had heard described innumerable times, as if it were the Promised Land. It lay on the other side of the Sierra—that high impenetrable range which formed the last and one of the most difficult barriers on the trail. So fearsome did it seem, that half the emigrants had decided to take a very lengthy detour around it to the north. It was as if God had constructed the journey to try the patience and test the devotion of those unfortunate enough to worship Him. And the Sierra was the crowning glory of the piece.

Having come south now for a few days, Daskin was pretty sure the Sierra was visible now to the east. That meant he was definitely on the other side. For the last few days he had suppressed any such thoughts, however, because he had crossed a lot of ranges before, only to find another range ahead. But when the trail began to turn west and descended for a couple of days without change—dipping into gullies and climbing over ridges—Daskin began to grow a little hopeful.

The trouble was, he was getting awfully weak. The little food he could find to eat was both meager and rotten. He had started to have dizzy spells. He had to rest more often and his legs were getting wobbly. His vision was becoming blurry. He had to rub his eyes continually and refocus on the trail ahead. He had long since discarded his shotgun and instruments, leaving him with only his notebooks and his dwindling supply of whiskey.

Then there was the snow....

Since morning a definite change had come into the weather, from merely threatening to actually inclement. The rain had dried up, and a dry powder had begun swirling around him in great white clouds, dancing in windy curlicues, blasting him from secret directions. In places it was already so thick on the trail that he sank into it up to his knees. His only hope now was to get in before his strength gave out, and his only hope of doing that lay in going all in. He didn't think he could survive another night—not in a storm like the one that had come on, not without shelter, food, warmth....

"Eighteenth. Commences with snow-storm. Wind S.E. Temp. sixteen degrees. The gale has drifted the snow very deep in places. Mind fuzzy. Must keep to trail. Saw something, then it wasn't there, like in a fever....

"Yes, I was right to get away. Why, Krup was nothing but an encumbrance, something completely useless on the trail, like a piano, or a statue of Bacchus. No, worse than useless. He was as troublesome as a baby. Fool

that I was, just like one of those mothers along the way, fretting and fuss-
ing as their babies became sick, continually begging to lay over just an-
other day or so. Of course! Why didn't I see it before? That was the genius
of the thing. What's more innocent-seeming than an infant, less likely to
arouse suspicion? Wasn't I always postponing what I might have accom-
plished in a couple of minutes, just so I could help Krup, who was no good
at anything and needed help all the time? And wasn't it out of deference to
Krup that we had turned right at the forks, in order to avoid the shorter
trail, the easier one, over the Sierra? Hadn't we made that decision against
our better judgment....

"Meridian, blizzard. Visibility near zero. Wind howling. My compan-
ion, at least, affords something civilized in the way of conversation during
these tedious hours. He is a distinguished elderly gentleman, frock-coated
and top-hatted, with a gilded walking stick and a solid gold pince-nez. He
has been to the mines, he informs me, and he confirms what I already have
heard, that gold nuggets are still to be picked up in the streams that flow
out of these very mountains, that gentlemen are still making their for-
tunes—he will not say with no effort—but with little drudgery for all that.
He brings the welcome news that, at present, I am only a few miles above
Lassen's Rancho, that fresh beef may be purchased there for fifty cents per
pound, flour for twenty-five. The same in the mines, or a little higher.
He discoursed at length upon the beauties of that Great Central Valley,
dwelling particularly upon the greenness of it, its numerous watercourses,
and its rich fertile soil. He has invited me to dine with him, when I should
find myself in San Francisco, at his mansion on Nob Hill, and to meet
his daughter, who is a renowned beauty. All in all, I have found my new
friend to be an ideal companion, and I cannot help but think that the time
will pass swiftly as we stroll the last few miles into civilization...."

As Daskin stumbled along into the drifting snow, the storm clouds
above him descended and engulfed the surrounding forest, tossing

the pine branches in furious howling. It no longer mattered that he couldn't see. The flurries soon wove themselves into a blinding white wall ahead, then swiftly engulfed him in a soft cocoon, into which he disappeared like a wriggling caterpillar.

FOUR DAYS LATER—after the storm had passed and the snow began melting, after one of the worst storms anyone could remember—a relief party set out from Lassen's *Rancho* to see if it could locate and bring in any of the emigrants who might still be straggling in on the trail. It was a bright, warm autumn day when the party of men on horses, leading pack mules laden with food, clothing, medicine, and camping gear, left the rancho and headed back up the trail.

About seven miles up, they found Daskin lying face down in a melting snow drift. They pulled out his stiff body and turned him over. His skin was ashen, his lips and fingernails blue, his eyelashes and beard coated with rime. In his right hand, he was clutching an empty whiskey bottle. They had to break the glass to remove it. He had evidently discarded the rest of his possessions, and therefore they were unable to identify him. In after years, if anyone remembered anything about him, it was the curious look of pleasure which he wore on his face when they found him.

Just when they were on the point of turning back, an exhausted and starving man came stumbling down the trail toward them, sobbing uncontrollably.

Krup had lost a good deal of weight, and several of his toes would have to be amputated. Otherwise, he was healthy. After recuperating at Lassen's *Rancho,* he continued on to the gold fields.

—*John Blanchard is a published and award-winning short story writer with an interest in the history of the American West. He divides his time between Oakland and Borrego Springs, California. His short stories have appeared in literary journals and the anthology* Best of the West 2010. *In his blog, John reflects on the writer's life and posts some of his short stories as well as excerpts from his novels. John is also a photographer. Some of his photos appear on his web site. www.johnblanchardwriter.com.*

COLOR OF GOLD

JAMES A. TWEEDIE

1850

WE COULD HAVE been shot or hung, or maybe something worse than that, but me and Beaton were at the end of our rope—which under the circumstances, probably isn't the best way to put it—but we knew we had to do something right quick or we were probably going to die anyway. But that part of the story comes later, and you'll hear it soon enough when I get to it.

Back when we were cubs, folks said that James Fletcher and Henry Beaton were two peas in a pod. We went to school together, climbed trees together, and fished the Atlantic with Beaton's daddy from when we was ten. Mackerel in the summer and bass in the winter and there was more of them fish than we could haul into the boat back in those days. We didn't know it till years later, but those were good times.

At Eighteen years, we got the itch. Too old to swim naked in the estuary and not enough money to buy a boat of our own. Neither of us wanted to up and join the Army or Navy, at least not unless both of us went in together. Beaton favored the Navy and I favored the Army, so since we couldn't agree on one or the other, we flipped a coin and gave it up when it landed in the dirt straight up on the edge.

We spent the winter of '49 and '50 gutting old Beaton's fish down at the city market and listening to tales about the gold folks were digging up halfway around the world in California. Tall tales, for sure. 'Specially the part about there being enough gold to make everyone rich for the next hundred years.

"Ain't gonna happen that way," I said to Beaton. "That gold's gonna run out sure as I'm tossin' fish guts into this here barrel. And even if we left now, it'll probably all be gone by the time we'get there."

"Mebbe," Beaton said with a grin. "But mebbe what's left will make us rich enough to buy a boat. Even if we scrape by, I bet we'll make more 'n we'll make in three years if we stay here. I say we sail to San Francisco and give it a go."

So, with nothing more than a nod from me, we say goodbye to our folks and sign on as crew for a clipper carrying barrels of rum, whiskey, and salted mackerel around the Horn.

It took three months for us to get from Charleston to San Francisco in the spring of 1850, and there's enough stories packed into that trip what could fill a book.

We were sicker from the stench of the cabin than from the thirty foot waves we fought at the Cape, but the mast and hull held together enough for us to plug the leaks as we headed north.

At San Francisco, we left the ship to rot next to what must have been a thousand others and headed toward what we hoped would be our personal piece of the Mother Lode.

Five days later, after stopping at Sutter's Fort for supplies, me and Beaton found ourselves up east of Coloma near Potter's Diggings.

Ten thousand men had gotten there before us and everything was so dug up and turned over it looked like something the Devil might have spit out of his mouth. Even the pine and oak trees had been cut down and the stumps blasted out of the ground to get at whatever gold might have been tucked up in the roots.

After two years, so much of the surface gold had been panned, sluiced, or sifted that investors began to pay men to either start burrowing into the ground like gophers or to channel water downhill for miles so they could wash hillsides away with what they call hydraulic mining. There was even talk of scraping and sucking up the river bottoms with dredges and vacuum pumps.

Most of that came later, but for Beaton and me, all we had was shovels, pans, a tent, and enough food to last us maybe two or three more days before we figured we'd starve to death.

We had spent our last dollar on the shovels and pans, and whatever hopes we had evaporated when we found that near every square foot of ground had been staked out as claims by men who, by now, were searching for gold fifty miles away.

We figured that finding new ground wasn't in the cards and neither of us wanted to sign on to dig into hell like at the Ophir mines up north of Mariposa. So that night we built a fire, boiled the last of our coffee, and tried to decide whether to jump a claim or trade the dream of getting rich for finding work in Sacramento.

Beaton wasn't particularly enthusiastic about either choice.

"Mebbe we should just call it quits and sign on with a ship to take us home the way we came."

"Mebbe," I said back at him. "But I saw a small boulder down by the creek that was just sitting there nearly all covered up in a heap of gravel."

Beaton didn't say anything so I kept talking.

"Tell you what," I said, "let's dig up that boulder in the morning

and see if we can turn it over to see what's underneath. If there's nothing there, let's head for Sacramento and find work enough to get us to
San Francisco and then home."

If Beaton hadn't liked the idea, he would have said something,
but since he just sat there staring at the fire, I knew his silence was as
good as a nod.

The next morning, I started shoveling the gravel while Beaton
tried panning some of it in the creek.

"Gold!" he cried, when he found the first sign of color.

"Shush!" I answered with a loud whisper. "There's mebbe fifty
men still hereabouts who'd be happy to shoot us dead for it, or to
string us up in Hangtown for taking what isn't ours."

But nothing came of it except for me to watch Beaton drop the
flecks into a small pouch he had carried all the way from home, hoping he would be filling it up twice a day with dust and nuggets when
he got to California.

Every pan of gravel he swished had some color in it, but even if
we'd panned day and night for a year, it wouldn't have amounted to
much—least not enough to get rich by it.

For a while, Beaton took his turn clearing the area around the
boulder while I tried my hand at panning. Then, when the gravel was
cleared, the two of us went to work digging out enough mud and sand
from the downhill side to roll the stone a few feet toward the creek.

The hole under the rock was filled with water but when I pushed
in my shovel it came up short as if it had hit another rock or a root
from some tree that wasn't there anymore.

"Blast!" I grunted as I reached my hand down into the water to
feel what I hit.

"It's another rock, sure enough. And sharp, too," I groaned as I
sucked blood from a torn fingertip.

"Well," Beaton said, as he picked up his shovel, "let's see if I can get it out."

By chance, his shovel slipped into a soft spot next to the rock and by throwing his weight onto the handle, the rock moved enough for the two of us to pry it loose.

Beaton reached into the water and what he pulled up was a chunk of quartz nearly a foot-and-a-half long and a good eight inches across. It was covered in dirt and mud but peeking through the muck I could see hints of gold gleaming in the light of the mid-morning sun.

Beaton carried it over to the creek where he rinsed it off, all the while trying his hardest to keep from yelling and bellowing over what he found.

"What is it?" I asked, unable to see anything but his back.

"It's what we came for," he said as he turned around and placed the surprisingly heavy rock in my hands.

Every crack and every depression in the rock was filled with gold—some of it all feathery as if it had once been tendrils of a minia-ture creeping vine touched by the King Midas of the Mother Lode. In other places the gold was thick and smooth. But the biggest surprise came when I turned it over and found the rock completely encrusted with an inch-thick layer of gold pure and soft enough for my finger-nail to have left a mark when I had first grasped it in my hands.

Without a word, I set the rock on the ground and, with Beaton at my side, we feverishly resumed digging in the hole as though we had but a few minutes left to live. We pulled up as much rock and gravel as we could reach until the bottom of the hole was nearly four feet below water level. We then examined and panned everything we had dug up but didn't find any more color than we had before.

In the end, we fell to the ground, exhausted, but still exhilarated by what we had found.

"Now what?" Beaton asked.

I started to answer by saying, "We cash in our chips and go home!" or some such thing, but I bit my tongue when I realized I had no idea what to do next.

"We can't go to an assayer," Beaton said, "'cause he'll want to know where we got it and show proof that we had claim to where we dug it up."

"Mebbe we can say that someone gave it to us?" I asked hopefully. "Or that we found it under a rock next to the road?"

"We'll be dead before morning, if we try to pull off a lie like that," Beaton said. "But whatever else we do, we gotta hightail it out of here pronto if we don't want to get caught picking some poor man's pocket."

I pulled off my shirt and wrapped it around our new-found fortune and the two of us ran back to our camp as fast as our tired legs and aching backs could go.

There, I tucked the rock into my bedroll, threw on my shirt, gathered up our gear, slung the bedroll over my shoulder and the two of us headed off toward Sacramento.

Before we had gone twenty feet, we heard the crack of a rifle shot from the direction of the creek followed by a voice that roared like a wounded grizz.

"Who from hell's been diggin' up my claim?"

The words seemed to echo endlessly through the still, sun-warmed air of a mid-June early afternoon.

"When I find 'im, I'll kill the bastard with my bare hands!"

But we were long gone before that grizz had a chance to track us down and finish us off.

Beaton and me, we didn't say anything for a long time.

Ten miles down the road I groaned out the words, "Can't buy food with a rock full of gold. Can't buy nothin'. Moneywise we're as poor as we were when we woke up this morning."

"True 'nuff," Beaton said. "So what are we gonna do? Carry that rock all the way back to Carolina?"

"If we have to, that's what we'll do," I answered. "But there's bound to be someone in San Francisco who'll buy it from us without asking any questions."

"Sure," Beaton said. "And he'll pay us less than half of what it's worth. I say, let's carry it back to Charleston, tell them we found it in California, and sell it at full value."

So, that's what we did, but after splitting the money, there was only enough for each of us to cover a year's worth of lost wages. So, for all our trouble, we just about broke even... except for becoming better friends than we had been before, and having a passel of stories to tell to our grandchildren.

But for that, we each had to first find a wife.

<hr>

—James A. Tweedie has lived in California, Utah, Scotland, Australia, Hawaii, and presently in Long Beach, Washington. He has published six novels, four collections of poetry, and one collection of short stories with Dunecrest Press. His award-winning stories and poetry have appeared in national and international anthologies including Frontier Tales *and* Saddlebag Dispatches *and his fantasy stories have received two Silver Certificate awards and one Honorable Mention from* Writers of the Future

He recalls moving from San Francisco to Logan, Utah, in 1979 and being both baffled and amused when he was asked, "What made you decide to move out West from California?"

In that moment, he learned that "the West" was not just a direction, but

a cultural space infused with traditions and tales embracing a heritage of mountain men, pioneers, Native Peoples, cowboys, homesteaders, prospectors, ranchers, railroads and a host of conflicts that stretched and expanded the United States into the country it is today.

His favorite corner of the West has been the Sierra Nevada where he has hiked and fly fished since he was old enough to walk.

BREAK

EDWARD A. GRAVES

EARLY MORNING SUN streamed through the window, a window he could only peek out of. Its light fell on his pant leg, and he watched as every grain of dirt and grime reflected as it floated off his boots and pants when he kicked his heel on the ground. It was a lovely morning, in a not so lovely place.

For some reason, he couldn't quite recollect for sure how long he and his boys had been holed up in this, their temporary fortress. But he did know that the length of time they'd been here didn't matter because today would be their last. His plan was set, it was as perfect as any plan could be under the circumstances, and he knew in his heart they'd make their break that day.

No doubt they'd ended up in a tough situation, somehow getting cornered up in this building, in Nevada City, California of all places. They were midwest boys, after all, just visiting for a bit. They'd held their own though and kept them at bay long enough for him to make the plan. He was their leader and was known far and wide for getting out of tough scrapes against seemingly impossible odds.

So well known in fact, that as he peeked out the window once again he couldn't help but notice that more than a few, both lawman and civilian, were milling about, all with an eye to his holdout—they were waiting to see whatever might come next.

"Sure got a lot of law out there," he said, not knowing which of his boys might hear or respond.

"That's a fact," he heard answered from another room. "Figure they got enough to deal with you?" the voice went on, with a snicker.

"We'll see partner, we will see," he answered back with a quiet snicker of his own.

He looked around the corner of the window frame once more and confirmed his thoughts—there were lots of people watching his way, many of them armed. The sight took his mind back to the day, he recollected, that had really started it all. The memory filled his mind.

It was late afternoon on their family farm, not a huge or prosperous place, but good enough to take care of his mom, dad, sister, and himself. He was the first to see the column of Union soldiers cresting the hill on the road that led past their house, and he called out an alarm to his family. His dad started walking at a fast pace toward him while signaling his mom and sister to go inside, and for him to be quiet. Accustomed to following their dad's lead, they all complied. His dad came up and put his arm around his son, standing tall, intending to meet the column with respect, without cowering. His dad had demanded that the family not take sides in the War Between the States, but rather just live their lives independent of the troubles. And while that had worked for them in the past, on that day, it had not. His mind raced over the events that followed. There had been no violence. The Union Army simply arrived, stated their needs and intentions, took the things that suited them, and moved on. He had wanted to fight them, but his dad had held him at bay with stern looks and the occasional squeeze on his shoulder. At the time he had thought his dad a coward, but as time passed he gained more and more respect for the strength his dad had shown that day. It was a fight he knew he could not possibly win in any other way than by total submission. As he remembered that event ending, he thought of the Union column moving away with so many of their goods now in their possession, his dad still standing tall and proud, but with the hint of a tear in his eye, and it occurred to him that this had become his true vision of strength and bravery. He also remembered that despite his dad's wishes and advice, the event had stirred anger in him that could not be denied. He joined the Confederate Army less than three weeks later, and that had defined his path leading straight up to this point.

A sharp, loud *bang* from somewhere beyond his vision brought him back to his present situation. The sound was familiar, but he could not quite place it. "Sounds like they're getting ready for us!" he said to whichever of his boys might hear. "You can bet on that," came an answer, "gonna be a hell of a fight." *Or did he say sight?* he thought. No matter, it was going to be both when he made his break. He looked out once again, kicked his heel against the boards of the floor, and watched more dirt float away. It didn't glisten quite as much as before because the sun was rising higher. The time for his move was growing closer, but it was still a ways off, and so, with nothing much else to do till then, he let his mind slip back to distant memories.

He thought briefly about the war, the parts he'd played, some wins and some losses, heroes and cowards, and the horrors he'd seen. He thought about the end and how he and several others had planned to surrender, but word came that half as many who tried to surrender to the Union Army were shot for their effort. And so he and several of his friends, while sitting around a campfire one night discussing what to do, made the fateful decision to go on with the fight, but now on their own terms and strictly for themselves. It started out simple enough—they robbed mostly stores, payrolls, and supply wagons of the Union Army, always sure to leave some of the spoils behind for any remaining Confederate sympathizers in the area. Their boldness grew and soon they were on to banks and trains with bigger rewards and much higher risks. The memories of the excitement and adrenaline of their exploits automatically raised his heartbeat and increased his blood flow to the point that he started anticipating those feelings to come from today's break. Then he began to remember the gunfights themselves, his own near misses and brushes with death, and the men he had shot. He took solace in the fact that he'd never killed or even seriously injured anyone who was not as hard and seasoned as himself, and who was not trying to shoot him first. He saw them fall in his memory, one by one, and with each he felt no guilt. Until came the memory of Bobby White, the killing that had put him in this fix, the one man he wished had not died by his hand. With Bobby's memory came a deep and sorrowful guilt that he knew, even in his subconscious, would not serve him well on this day. He knew he couldn't bring Bobby back, there was no way to pull that bullet back, but he vowed that once free of this place he would find another place where he could lead a peaceful life.

A loud *bang* came from somewhere out on the street, once again bringing him back to the here and now. *What the hell is that?* he thought, but was still unable to place it. *Probably setting up some barricades to block my escape, but it won't be enough. Others have tried that before,* he thought on with a confident expression on his face. Nobody had ever stopped them, or even resisted for long, when he and his boys were in full fight. They were a force to be reckoned with. He looked at the sun, the time was getting closer, and their plan was soon to unfold. No need to discuss it further now, it was set and everyone knew what to do and when to do it. He squatted down and stood up again, shook his arms out, and stomped his feet again, all just to keep the blood flowing and muscles loose. More dust floated off of him as he did so. *Gonna get me a bath and fresh clothes when this mess is done,* he thought—this time he even let a little laugh escape his lips. He looked out on the street once more and noticed even more people were out and about, many with guns, many without, most watching in his direction, waiting to see his move. He squinted up at the sun one more time, carefully gauged the time, and decided he needed to relax just a bit longer. The timing, after all, was critical. Unfortunately though, try as he might, the memory of Bobby made its way back into his mind.

Bobby had joined up with them about a year ago. He was a good kid and damned fine in a fight, but he had a problem with whiskey, and the whiskey brought problems to him. The whole reason they'd ended up in this town was that Bobby was originally from Nevada City and he made a strong case that it would be a great place for them to let the law cool, and have a very good time. Their pockets were full and the law was on them so they decided to make their way here to see his family, on one condition... if they were going to lay low, Bobby had to curb his in town drinking, he had a reputation for such things. He agreed. Bobby's family welcomed them, let them all stay, and fed them well. They maintained a low profile in town and enjoyed a very nice, and welcome, break from the trail. But, it was an exciting city, and Bobby was well known and liked in a few local establishments. And so after more than a few peaceful days, as they were making plans to return to their preferred territory, it was decided it would be safe to spend one night in town to let Bobby and their new friends give them a very private, sort of going away party, on their way out.

And it was a very fine night indeed, up to a point. The saloon put out extra food for the gathering, the piano player had been in fine form, and of course the beer and whiskey flowed freely. It was somewhere around midnight he guessed, when he first saw that look in Bobby's eyes, that look that he'd come to know meant trouble was brewing. Subtly he got word to the rest of the boys, and they all recognized the same—it was time for them to get out, and Bobby along with them. At first, Bobby just shrugged off the suggestion that they leave, downing another shot of whiskey in the doing. Then the inevitable happened as Bobby got into an argument with one of his long time friends and a scuffle broke out. What happened next happened, it seemed, in the blink of an eye. He and the boys had separated Bobby from his adversary, he taking Bobby himself. But Bobby had spun from his grasp and turned on him. "You ain't bossin' me in my own goddamned town!" Bobby shouted at him.

"I'm not bossin' you Bobby, I'm askin', as your friend," he'd answered with his hands outreached, palms up, so as not to be confrontational. This had seemed to calm Bobby for a moment, but the moment passed.

"You tell us where to go, when to eat, who to hit, how to hide, and every other goddamned thing out there. Out there." Bobby gestured outward. "But not in here!" And he pointed to the ground. "In here, I'm the boss and I say I've had just about enough of your bossin'!" Bobby was in his blind rage now, and he knew that what would come next could not be predicted.

He had simply stood there, hands out, palms up, silently hoping that somehow Bobby would stand down. And once again, Bobby seemed to relax just a bit. "Awww, hell," Bobby said. "What am I gonna do …shoot you?" Thinking he saw a moment of opportunity, he'd stepped slowly forward. But in a flash that look of rage returned and Bobby had drawn on him. "Believe I will, come to think of it. That'll make me the boss, here, and out there."

Against all of his instincts, he did not draw in return. He knew he was far faster and much more accurate than Bobby, but they'd rode together, shared bread and blood together, been brothers on the trail, and so he did not draw. Rather, he simply continued to smile, hands outstretched, palms up, and said, "Then shoot me Bobby, I could use the rest." He had never been more stunned in his entire life than when, an instant later, he watched flame explode from the end of Bobby's pistol and he felt a bullet tear through his shoulder. Still, he maintained his composure. Experience told him the wound was relatively minor. He staggered back a few steps but regained his footing and turned back to Bobby with hands still outstretched. "Okay, son, you got me, I'm shot, and you win. Now let's call it a night and we'll ride outta here together."

But Bobby wasn't done, he was still holding his pistol on him and the rage in his eyes flared on. "Oh, hell no," Bobby said. "Only one man calls me son, and he taught me to always finish what I start." He felt the dread of what he realized for the first time he might have to do. He stood fast as Bobby pulled back the hammer on his pistol. He tried to use his eyes to communicate, please don't, you know what'll happen. But Bobby was past seeing, his eyes blinded by rage. His many years of experience, in battle and showdown alike, focused his own eye on the knuckle of Bobby's trigger finger. He saw it go from red to white as pressure was applied.

There was no thought, no time to think. Before he knew what had happened, his own gun had been drawn, aimed, fired, and re-holstered. He saw the rage leave Bobby's eyes, a wisp of smoke rising up from the hole just above and between Bobby's eyes. He seemed to look at him for just a moment with a look of bewildered betrayal, and then simply fell backward, hitting the floor with a thud "Damn it, Bobby, damn it," he said.

And that's when he heard from somewhere in the gathering, "No, damned you!" and another shot rang out in his direction, missing wildly, as amateur shots tended to do. In the next few moments it was as if they were back in full war battle with guns firing from, and in, every direction. Of course, with their experience they were by far the more formidable force, but someone must have got a lucky shot in because he felt an instant of pain at the back of his head.

He had woken up here, in this very room, some hours later. That was when he came to determine that he'd been pistol whipped from behind, but his boys had gathered him up and made a successful break from the saloon—then a barrage of fire from the townspeople had driven them into this building, where they'd been holed up ever since. He thought of Bobby, his friend and comrade, falling backward with that hole in his head—a hole he'd put there—and the madness that ensued. And now they were in this sanctuary from which they would have to escape.

Bang! That same loud bang brought him back to the moment. He shook his head and sighed over the guilt he felt over having killed Bobby. *After this,* he thought, *after this I'm living clean.* He squinted one more time at the sun. It was time.

"You ready?" he heard from another room.

"Damn right," he answered back. "Take your positions boys, I'm done with this place."

As planned, he'd watched the morning from his good vantage point, but it was not where he'd make his move from. And so quietly, he made his way to his appointed position for the break. He knew he'd win, but he also knew it was going to be a fight, and so for the briefest of moments as he moved along, he thought of other things. His dad, the definition of strength and bravery. His mom, from whom he'd learned love and respect. And that barmaid in Amarillo who had so wanted him to take her to San Francisco to live a peaceful life. *Maybe I'll go find her and do just that after this,* he thought.

But there was no more time for thought, it was time for action. He shook out his legs and arms once more and rocked his head in a circular motion—he was loose, he was ready, every sense was spiked. He waited for the signal. Every muscle tensed as he prepared himself, and then it started.

He felt the air below his feet as he jumped. He heard that loud bang again, and this time he recognized it. He looked for a brief second and saw all the faces that had come to watch his break. He was above them, but falling fast. He looked back and recognized his vantage point from the morning, it was the jail. There was an instant of pain, similar, but different, from what he'd felt at the end of the fight in the saloon. This pain was quicker though, in his neck this time, more severe, and came with a crack that seemed to fill his ears.

He'd done it again. He'd made his break. He was free. His legs twitched a time or two, but by then, he was already back on the trail, headed toward San Francisco to find that lady. He was without fear or worry, never to fear, fight, or worry again.

The break was clean.

—*Edward A Graves is the author of Sully's American West. He moved to Oklahoma in 1986 where he became infatuated with America's Old West. In his first published work, a two volume series, his fictional character Sully gives his firsthand, historically accurate, account of every famous and infamous event and character that defined America's Old West.*

In "The Break," he turns to pure fiction as the leader of a gang of outlaws that seek refuge in Nevada City, California during the gold rush, only to be caught up in an unexpected fight for their lives. He is well known for evading capture after having made several successful breaks from seemingly impossible odds. The Break he makes this time is truly unforgettable...

To learn more about Edward A Graves, Sully's American West, *and his other western writings please visit his website at Sully's American West and join his 1500+ followers on Sully's American West*

VAGRANTS ON A MOUNTAIN PASS

JESS MINSTER

THE SMALL COMMUNITY of Blanch was, indeed, bleached white. All year round, snow would come down from the sky and paint the world with a horrible, bleak blanket. It was a community built on the backs of miners, people who had come West to find their fortunes in the cold rock beneath the colder ice. The population of the town never broke one hundred.

During one particularly heavy blizzard, a man came walking into the narrow, steep streets of the town, covered from head to toe in furs, just as everyone else in the town. The town was absolutely dead in the darkness of night, in the gray whirlwind of endless snow. Just about the only thing the man could see was a single lantern inside of a window about thirty paces ahead of him. Pulling his uneasy horse through the icy tempest made the thirty paces feel like a hundred. Eventually, however, the man had trudged all the way up to the partially-buried front door of the wooden house. Knowing that the wind was too loud for anyone to hear him shout or knock normally, he slammed his fist into the door almost as hard as he could.

After a short while, the door opened. Standing there in the slight warmth of the indoors was a short black man with some silver teeth, replacing the many he had lost. "Whoa there!"

"Outta the way!" The man shouted, pushing past the other, rushing toward the raging fire on the other end of the big room almost instinctively. Barely even noticing the ten or so other people in the room getting their guns out at this seemingly aggressive action, the man quickly ripped off his gloves and put his purple, bloated hands close to the fire.

"What do you think you're—?" one white man hollered, before seeing what the man was doing.

After a spell, most of the men in the house lowered their weapons, and the man who entered from the cold turned to see the vast number of them. The only sound the man made was that of shallow, excited breathing.

"Quite a strange mix, you are!" the man said, pulling off his snow-caked coat to reveal a poncho. "Call me Jeremias."

The angered white man, a fellow with long, blond hair, still held his shotgun close. "What makes you so sure we're welcoming to strangers, Mex'can?"

"Whether you're welcoming or not is not the question," Jeremias responded. "I've come in from the cold. I'm sure you folk don't want no trouble, so..."

"Like hell we don't want no trouble! Why are you here?"

"Maybe I'm just a poor man looking for a little gold, friend." Jeremias rubbed his hands together to try to generate more heat.

"Mex'can, you'd best run along."

"I ain't Mexican. I'm Guatemalan, and I'm afraid that if you don't want to kill me then there's little choice but for you to let me stay here till the weather gets better."

The white man pushed Jeremias slightly back, away from the fire. "Besides, your horse is coming in tracking mud all over the place, get it out of here!"

"Look," Jeremias said, putting his hands up diplomatically, "This is Blanch, California, isn't it?"

"Yes."

"Then I'm here for work. I don't know who runs things, but I figured the only house around with a lamp must be a good place to start my search."

"Listen. Get your horse out of here! We can talk about this when you get back. The stables are just behind this house."

"I don't mean to be presumptuous, but you folks look like a hungry sort. I came up here with a bit of money. Twenty dollars, all I've got to my name." Jeremias took out a soggy stack of dollar bills and continued, "I'll give half of it to whoever wants to go out and hitch up my horse and the other half to whoever owns this place to let me sleep here tonight."

The men all paused to look at one another. As a general trend among the men, most looked toward one dark figure reclined back in a chair in the corner of the room. Jeremias tried to not follow their glances.

"Very well," the blond man said after a moment. "Give me the money. We'll split it amongst ourselves." He stuck his hand out toward Jeremias.

"You gonna be hitching my horse?" Jeremias held his hand back so the blond man couldn't grab the money.

"No. But give it to me."

For a second, Jeremias considered protesting this, but he figured that it was all the same to him if his horse got taken care of. He gave the blond man his money.

"Thank you kindly. Walton, you go out'n put his horse away, mm?"

"Sure thing." A redheaded man stepped over and started for the still-open door. He grabbed Jeremias' horse's reins and guided it out of the doorway, back into the snow. He shut the door after him.

"I appreciate this, friend," Jeremias said, taking out a tobacco pipe. "Does anyone have any matches? Mine got soaked."

A match struck in the corner of the room. Jeremias looked to see the dark figure in the chair, fur-clad, holding a lit match. "Come over and get it, mister," the dark figure said with a rasp.

Jeremias stepped over to the man in the corner chair. He was covering the match so no draft would put it out. The only feature Jeremias could see of the man's face was a scar on his chin.

"Thank you, sir." The Guatemalan held his pipe out and the dark figure lit it.

━━━━━━━━━━━━━

ONCE WALTON CAME back, Jeremias was sitting in a rocking chair right next to the fireplace with all his things placed out to dry nearby, guns included.

"Heh, really took him in like one of our own, huh?" Walton said, looking at the blond.

"He gave us all his money, so why send him out in the snow? We ain't that kind of band!"

"Band?" Jeremias spoke up, raising an eyebrow at the white man's phraseology.

"Yes, yes... We're private miners. That's why we all share these quarters," the dark figure said quickly.

"Hm. They don't segregate your men?" Jeremias motioned to the short black man near the doorway with his pipe.

"Why... no," the black man said. "Norm, tell him."

"We ain't got enough space for that up here," Norm said.

"Very well. Why do you folks hold your guns like that?"

Norm looked down at his hands. He was carrying his shotgun more like a club than a gun—the same as the rest of the men. Suddenly, Norm corrected his grip on the gun and stepped toward Jeremias, offended. "You're a curious man, hombre."

"Didn't mean to offend you," Jeremias said.

"We... we don't have any ammunition," Norm said reluctantly.

"No ammunition? You mean to tell me, in a whole group of miners stocked with a gun per man doesn't have a single bullet?"

"Well—" Norm looked at the man in the corner without thinking.

Jeremias looked back at the figure. "You're an exception?"

"We're not discussing this further. We're not discussing anything further," the dark figure said. "Jeremias, you're free to stay. You're not free to question with such scrutiny as you have."

"Norm," Jeremias started, looking back at Norm. "You've got loose lips, son."

"'Son.' Haven't heard that shit since I left Missouri."

"Missouri!" Jeremias exclaimed. "You've come quite a way."

"Norm!" The man in the corner shouted, his voice cracking a bit. "Shut your damn mouth!"

Norm sat down on the floor below him, surrendering to the dark figure's whim.

"And Jeremias," the Figure said, taking out a revolver, "You'd best stop now. You don't want to go any further."

"Very well."

"KEEP OFF," JEREMIAS said, leaning forward in the rocking chair, just awoken by Norm reaching for one of Jeremias' two pistols, which he had kept in his gun belt for safekeeping during his sleep. He cocked one of them, aiming at the man.

Norm stumbled backwards, surprised by Jeremias' light slumber.

The man in the corner was awoken by the sound of his men stirring. Hearing the dark figure move, Jeremias grabbed his second revolver, cocking it and aiming it at the scarred man as he creaked the chair around to see him. Everyone froze, their hands on their weapons—still holding them inappropriately. The dark figure's hand hovered over his holster.

"I've been thinking," Jeremias started. "Why weren't there any other lamps in this town? Why couldn't I find anyone else? Why did I feel a certain danger upon coming into this cabin? And why, against all odds, was the state of Missouri ringing such a bell...? Well, I'll tell you. Before I left San Francisco, I happened to read a newspaper. Right there, plain as day, the infamous Barley City Gang, spotted heading into the Sierra Nevada Mountains. I had heard some stories about them before, and heard some information about the leadership of the gang. Some information that might be able to lure an injured snake out of its hole."

"The hell are you getting at?" The dark figure croaked.

"Somehow, in my innocent search for wealth, I'd come across a desperate gang on the run, having killed everyone in a tiny mining town and hid out in a ramshackle little house on a mountain. I know, boys. I know that you ain't no mountaineers or prospectors. You're nothing better than some vagrants on a mountain pass. I put it all together during the silent moments before I fell asleep. See, I still allowed myself to sleep. Not because I was just so tired, but because I don't want no trouble."

"No trouble—I'm gonna bash your ugly face in, *señor!*" Norm said, twitching in his boots.

"We don't want any trouble either," the man in the corner said. "Put your guns down and stop talking crazy."

"I'm afraid I can't do that. I know you'll blast me away at any moment because you've got no scruples with killin'. But I'm telling you this, Lucy Cole. I've got information that you might find interesting about your beloved MacCray."

"MacCray?" The dark figure sputtered, breaking his voice for a moment, revealing the softer voice of a woman hidden under pounds of bearskin and scar tissue.

"That's right," Jeremias reassured. "I read about the old leader of this outfit as well. Your husband, Cole."

Cole stood up abruptly, her hand still hovering over her holster. "I could put a bullet between your eyes for bringing up—"

"Think before you say, woman! I know what's become of your husband. No one else here—hell, no one else for the next fifty miles—could tell you that."

Cole's scarred face scrunched up in anger. She spat on the floor.

"I've got twelve shots, if not more, if I can get a reload in. You've got, what? Ten?"

"I only need one shot."

"As do I. For each of you."

Norm wound his arm back, preparing to swing his shotgun at Jeremias. Jeremias shot, then cocked that revolver once more.

Norm fell to the ground, slipping on a rug on the way down.

Cole drew her gun, but Jeremias shot first. Cole toppled back into her chair, which slid away and caused her to fall to the floor as well.

The rest of the bandits swarmed Jeremias, who quickly shot as many of them that decided to come toward him. Within less than a minute, the house became silent, with the rush of wind outside becoming the only noise that could be heard.

Every shot had been a killshot, except for—

"You son of a bitch!" Cole growled, blood dripping from her mouth. She had dropped her pistol on the way down to the floor, and now she was too weak to grab it.

Jeremias stood from the chair, glancing over the entire house, seeing no movement except for that of Cole. He turned toward her and walked her way. He slid out some bullets from his bandelier and started loading one of his revolvers.

"I could kill you right now, Cole," Jeremias said. "But I ain't no killer. Not no more." He shut the cylinder of his revolver and aimed it at Cole's head, then standing above her. "I tried to leave this type of thing behind, south of the border. But look at what you've done... You done dragged me back into it." He cocked the revolver's hammer. "I could bring you in alive, but that would be a waste of energy, wouldn't it? It counts a lot up here."

"Fuck you," Cole said with disdain.

"But I also figure, why should you die not knowing what happened to your sweet MacCray?"

Cole looked into Jeremias' eyes, a million different emotions flashing across her face.

"He was caught in a border town somewhere between Arizona and California. The authorities are trying to bring you out by letting him live. I'm sure you're smart enough to know that, even if you did come out, they'd still have the both of you hang in the end."

Cole swallowed some of her own blood and saliva.

Jeremias fired.

The next day, after some rest, Jeremias inspected the rest of the town. About an hour into this strenuous venture, he stumbled across a shack across the road from the house. Inside, there was a large stockpile of cloth bags. While some of the bags were not labeled, others read, *Property of the Bank of San Francisco.* Inside the labeled bags, Jeremias discovered the entirety of the Barley City Gang's final score. And inside the unlabeled bags, he found many loads of unprocessed gold—what must have belonged to the poor folks that ran this town before the Barley City Gang came in and before they had the chance to do anything with it. Before, there had been the question of how Jeremias would come across his fortune. Now, there was the question of the gold. How was he to get it down from this mountain? And with whose help?

———

—Jessica Minster is a maverick author and poet based out of Northern Arizona who has written many short stories, poetry collections, and novels in the over ten years she has been writing creatively. Her process is not unlike an exorcism, in which she furiously channels the voices within her to the page. She tends to stick to darker, more psychological, and more subversive types of projects. Interested in a wide variety of genres and styles, Jessica enjoys experimenting with literary fiction just as much as pulpy crime fiction, cerebral science fiction, and more. She has been published in Defunct Magazine, Northern Arizona University's Interdisciplinary Writing Showcase, Guilty Crime Story Magazine, *among others, and has had her work produced into a podcast episode by Scare You To Sleep. Recently she has interned for* Frontier Poetry *as a reader for the publication and has self published a collection of poetry, an issue of a literary magazine, and an experimental novella online.*

Back From the Trading Post by Frank Tenney Johnson

DEATH ❀ A DREAM

CHERYL PIERSON

"BETTER RIDE DOWN into the canyon and round up any strays, Jimmy. Take Aldous with you."

Ben Halston casually reached into his shirt pocket for a quirlie and lucifers. His steel gray eyes arrested Jimmy's wandering attention as he lit the cigarette. Ben shook the flame from the match and smiled at Jimmy's poorly concealed distaste for the job he'd been directed to do.

"If you're going to take this spread over someday, Jim, you're gonna have to do a lot of jobs that you *could* delegate. The men don't respect a boss that won't jump in and do anything he tells another man to do. Part of bein' a good foreman—or an owner." He gave Jimmy a knowing nod. "An' that's what I expect you'll be one day, with you and Bethy gettin' married next month."

"Yes, sir." Jimmy gave him a respectful nod and began to turn his horse, but Ben's voice stopped him.

"A man needs to know everything he can about the men who work for him, Jim. Really, for everyone close to him—even family."

Ben rode closer. "It's important. The more you know, the better off you are. Remember that."

"Yes, sir."

———————⊱⊰———————

JIMMY RODE AWAY to find Aldous and do the old man's bidding. Ben was always trying to impart tidbits of wisdom in his folksy way, and Jimmy was sick of listening to it. Ben's way of doing things was much different from Jimmy's own. Not that Ben's way was wrong, Jimmy thought, it was just outdated.

Once he collected the taciturn Aldous and they'd wordlessly headed for the canyon, Jimmy's thoughts drifted.

Beth would be his wife soon. And after that, at some point, as Ben had said, Jimmy Franklin would become the owner of the Circle H spread. And when the old man eventually died, why, this place would become the Circle F. Jimmy smiled at the thought. If he and Beth were lucky enough to have several boys, one of them would keep the brand alive for the next generation, and maybe even the one after.

Beth. The horse seemed to almost lose his footing on the path as Jimmy conjured her up in his mind. Beth would be a good, dutiful wife. Having been raised on the ranch, she knew what would be expected of her—the chores, the loneliness of the range, and the extra things that most ranch wives knew how to do—from doctoring, to canning, to growing a garden...

Beth was a woman of many talents. And she was easy on the eyes... Jimmy grinned outright at that thought.

He'd loved her since the day he'd met her. He'd been in third grade, she in first. His little eight-year-old self had been much more knowledgeable in the ways of the world than shy, soft-spoken Beth Halston.

But the minute he'd laid eyes on her, he knew he wanted to marry her someday. And now, it was expected—by everyone who knew them.

"There's a couple," Aldous said, breaking into Jimmy's thoughts. "I'll get after 'em."

"No, just wait, Aldous. Let's get all the way to the end of the canyon and make a sweep coming back this way. Save us some time."

Aldous shrugged. "Your call, boss."

Jimmy chuckled. "Not yet, Aldous. I'm not the boss—at least not for a while."

———————◆———————

BY THE TIME they'd rounded up all the strays and driven them back to the mouth of the canyon, both men were aggravated by the uncooperative ways of the beeves they'd gathered.

Hot and short-tempered, Aldous rode on ahead, but suddenly seemed to falter and stop at something he'd seen off the trail. He motioned to Jimmy to stop the animals that were trying to leave trail and head for the nearby lake, but Jimmy was ready to be done with this job and get back to the ranch.

He pushed onward as if he hadn't seen Aldous frantically motioning to him. The very thought of getting cleaned up and having a good meal with Beth and the Halston family—and maybe stealing a kiss or two—dominated his thoughts as he rode on.

He caught up to Aldous, but before he could say anything, Aldous gave him a mournful look such as Jimmy had never seen, then glanced shamefacedly away as Jimmy came abreast of him.

"Aldous? What—"

"Yonder," Aldous said in a whisper, pointing half-heartedly toward the small, secluded lake that was lined with evergreen trees.

Some of the stragglers had again started to drift toward the water, and Jimmy made to follow them, but Aldous laid a hand on Jimmy's arm.

"Look again there, young'un. *Careful,* this time. Don't git yerself murdered."

This time, Jimmy did look. *Hard.*

Beth... and... another man. An Indian. And it was someone he recognized. *Cochise's nephew.*

They all called him Bobby Blanket, the whites. A way of removing any kind of pride he might assume—*if* they'd respected him enough to call him by his real name. A name none of them could even pronounce correctly.

Part white himself, Bobby traded and mingled with the settlers of Cochise County and was congenial—until he looked at a person dead-on with the coldest steel in his eyes behind the smile he wore. A look that let someone know he would kill if he had the chance. A look that said, "Watch your back. I'll be there—and I know a thousand ways to kill."

And here was Bobby Blanket... swimming with Beth. *His* Beth. And she was smiling up at Bobby with a loving light in her eyes that Jimmy swore he'd never seen from her in his entire life. And right now, he'd give his life to see that smile on Beth's lips, the glow around her, the adoration in her eyes—if only all that could be *his* for just one second.

But she didn't know Jimmy was anywhere within a hundred miles of her. She was a woman in love...with an Indian. *With Bobby.*

For the first time it hit Jimmy that it didn't matter if Bobby was Indian, Chinese, or white. He was a rival, and he'd already won from the looks of things.

"Want me to kill him?" Aldous asked quietly. He spit tobacco juice onto the dry earth. Jimmy's horse shied, and he cut Aldous a hard glance.

"No, I don't want you to kill him. You want to bring the entire Apache Nation down on us here? He ain't worth it." Under his breath, he muttered, "And neither is she."

"Well...what, then?"

Jimmy pressed his lips together and turned away from the scene. "Round up those stragglers and let's head for home."

"Yes, sir, boss."

Jimmy shrugged away the irritation he felt at Aldous for being here to witness the scene. He needed to be calm. "Aldous—you keep your damn mouth *shut!* You hear?"

Aldous gave a faint smile and tipped his hat. "Yes, *boss—*"

"Stop calling me that," Jimmy snarled.

"Mm-hmm...guess I *should,* at that." Aldous was already headed for the strays, and Jimmy tamped down the anger he felt at the older man's smug attitude.

He forced himself to look away from the lake where his fiancée was swimming with another man. His rival. A man he wasn't sure he could defeat in this particular battle.

He made himself get the horse moving and helped Aldous round up the cattle, slowly driving them to the canyon entrance where they plodded up the trail to higher ground.

———◆———

JIMMY WASN'T SURE how he got back to Circle H land, but he should have known his horse would always find his way back...even if Jimmy was woolgathering about what he'd witnessed earlier between Beth and Bobby.

It was coming up on supper time, and Beth had not come home yet. He was of a mind to go and wait for her, catch her as she came riding in bold as brass with a satisfied cat-who-ate-the-canary smile on her face.

But it was enough that he knew. And so did Aldous, if he needed any confirmation.

No, he'd bide his time. Pain numbed him so that he could barely think, until the hurt gave way to rage.

It was just an expectation that his and Beth's wedding would take place next month and that Jimmy would ease into ownership of the Circle H. Could he give all that up now? Break it off with Beth at this late date? Make himself the laughingstock of Cochise County?

Jimmy headed toward the river to clean up before going in for the evening meal. As he dismounted and knelt beside the clear water, his reflection surprised him. He looked distraught...completely unraveled. Ben would see his roiling emotions written plainly all over him—the deep valleys of worry in his face, the hard line of compressed lips, the furrow of his brows, and the choppy motions of a carnival automaton as he moved. Worst of all, the hurt and rage that flashed in his eyes no matter where his gaze happened to fall.

He loved Beth too much to allow her to go to that—*that savage.* He'd vowed to give Beth anything she wanted in life—*anything.*

Anything but Bobby Blanket.

He'd be damned if he'd allow Bobby to step in and take this spread away from him. Ben wouldn't allow that, either. Ben doted on his only child, but he would not tolerate handing over all he'd worked for these long years to a half-Chiricahua Apache Indian. *This,* Jimmy knew.

He washed his hands and face clean of the sweat and trail dust, allowing his thoughts to clear.

Beth still belonged to Jimmy... if he could be content in marrying her for the position of being her husband, the heir to the Circle

H—and always know he was not the love of Beth's life. It had never occurred to him that she might fall in love with someone else.

Hot, shameful tears stung his eyes. Disappointed, hurt, and truly shocked at what he'd seen earlier, he was appalled to realize he was near breaking down and bawling.

He gave himself a stern emotional shake. He was not a woman. He was a man, and not the first to ever have an unfaithful partner. To be honest with himself, he and Beth were not *really* partners. She'd only just turned twenty. She'd agreed to marry him, but now that he thought about it, she'd seemed reluctant when she'd given him her answer.

The answer that had been expected of her by everyone. It had never occurred to Jimmy that Beth might not be in love with him.

He stood by the riverbank, his fists clenched, thoughts racing.

He would confront her. But he had to think about how he'd go about it. Beth was very headstrong and used to having her own way.

The adoring look in her beautiful brown eyes as she'd gazed up at Bobby—*oh, lord. She'd not had any clothes on.* At the time, it hadn't registered, but now, Jimmy realized there had been no undergarment straps on her shoulders—her sun-kissed skin had been completely bare.

This time, Jimmy couldn't help himself. He staggered backward a step and sat down. The tears came suddenly. He might not be a baby, but dammit, he felt like one right now. Helpless, hurting, and hollow.

He cursed Beth through his sobs and would have screamed those curses aloud to the skies, but for being heard by the other hands—or worse, by Ben Halston himself. And then, he'd be shot, or worse. The old man loved Beth more than anything else in this world. He'd never believe… Jimmy wiped his eyes with the heels of his hands. *He'd* not believe it either, if he had not seen it for himself.

Darkness began to gather. There was nothing to do but go on up to the house for supper before it got any later. By now, Beth would be back. It was time to see if he could face her.

AS JIMMY ENTERED through the front door, Beth came in from the kitchen. She'd slipped in the back way, he realized, and just in the nick of time, as Ben was waiting at the dinner table.

Jimmy graciously seated Beth to the right of her father, and then walked around the table to sit across from her, to Ben's left.

There was an extra place set beside Beth, and Jimmy felt unreasoning anger boil up inside. Rightfully, by this point in time, he should be the one sitting beside Beth rather than across from her.

Just then, the front door opened tentatively, and they all turned to see who entered.

"Bobby!" Beth couldn't contain the happy excitement in her voice.

Anger washed over Jimmy and clutched his heart as Bobby came in.

"Come on in, Bob. We were just getting dinner on the table," Ben said jovially, acknowledging Bobby's entry just as the cook, Alberta, brought in a steaming platter laden with pot roast and vegetables.

She nodded at Bobby as she sailed past him and set the platter down in the middle of the table, close to the end where the diners were seated.

"Evenin', Mister Bobby," she said with a smile. "You have a seat here by Miss Beth, and I'll bring in the rolls. What would you care to drink?" She stopped to look at him. "We have tea, lemonade, or some mighty fine water."

Bobby stopped to hang his hat on the rack, then turned toward Alberta and gave her a polite nod. "Thank you, Miss Alberta. I'll have tea, if you don't mind."

"I'll bring it right in. You just have a seat."

Jimmy watched as Beth squirmed in her chair. Bobby pulled out the chair beside Beth and slid into it with a nod at Ben.

"Mister Halston. Miss Beth." He glanced at Jimmy. A goading light came into his obsidian eyes, though his expression never changed, remaining set with a slight smile. "Mister Franklin."

Jimmy managed to keep a stone-faced stare in place and give a silent nod of greeting as Bobby sat beside Beth in the chair that should rightfully be his. He swallowed hard and tried to keep the hatred from his eyes. Bobby, being half-Indian, would see that, and Jimmy couldn't allow *that* to happen.

Jimmy couldn't help but glance at Beth. The love she felt for Bobby was palpable. Unknowingly, she moved closer to Bobby, who in turn, distanced himself by an inch or two by scooting his chair forward and to the side.

"Let's say grace," Ben commanded.

"Oh, Papa, let me," Beth asked prettily.

"Of course, sweetheart," Ben replied with a doting smile.

They all bowed their heads, Jimmy seething inside as he tried to look calm.

"Thank You, oh, Lord, for this very *special* day. Thank You for the food we are about to partake of through the blessings of Your bounty. Thank You for letting us all be gathered here in peace and safety beneath this roof. Again, thank You for this most *wonderful* day. In Jesus' name we pray, amen."

Her quiet voice, so serenely, honestly thankful for the day that had ruined Jimmy's life, ignited his wrath. He clenched his hands in his lap, muttering 'amen' before he dared raise his eyes. His gaze immediately met Beth's, and she hurriedly glanced away as if she'd been slapped.

"Bethy, would you mind dishing me up some of that roast and

vegetables?" Ben asked, handing Beth his plate. He glanced at Jimmy. "Better'n passin' that big ol' platter all around the table."

"Of course, Papa." Beth deftly took his plate and piled it with food, then held it out to him.

He smiled and winked at her as he took it. "Thank you, dearest."

She gave the serving spoon to Bobby, who scooped some of the meat and vegetables onto his plate and shifted the spoon back to Beth.

Jimmy sat quietly as Beth made to hand the spoon to him.

"I'll wait till you've been served, Bethy," Jimmy said in a quiet tone.

Her head shot up, and they stared at one another for a split second before Jimmy added casually, "Ladies first. A man always takes care of his woman before himself."

He nodded at the food. "Go ahead, sweetheart. Your man is starving after rounding up all those strays in the canyon."

She'd started to put a small portion of the meat on her plate, but stopped and stiffened at his words.

Bobby looked at Jimmy and asked, "Did you have quite a few stragglers to round up?"

"Sure did," Jimmy replied. "Over close to Evergreen Lake."

Beth dropped the big serving spoon as she moved it back to the platter. It plopped into the gravy and vegetables, splattering a few droplets of gravy onto the tablecloth.

"Here, honey, I'll get it," Jimmy said in a solicitous tone, reaching for the spoon.

He dished up a hearty portion onto his plate, giving her a smile. "You okay?"

She nodded. "Yes. Yes...it just slipped."

The blood had drained from her face, but Jimmy continued.

"Yes. Things do that sometimes." Jimmy took a bite of his food. "Slip, I mean."

"Pass those rolls up here, Bobby," Ben directed. "I tell you, Alberta makes the best rolls you've ever tasted, doesn't she, Jim?"

Jimmy nodded, not unaware of Ben's attempt to change the subject and put the conversation right again. Had Ben also somehow known of Beth's meeting with Bobby in the lake? His mind clouded, trying to accept what he'd witnessed this afternoon.

"One of these days, soon, I expect this house will ring with children's laughter, and what a happy day that will be for us all, right, Jim? Beth?"

As Jimmy was called back to the present from his musings by Ben's comment, Beth briefly met his eyes and blushed at her father's bald statement.

Jimmy tried to hold Beth's gaze, enjoying her obvious discomfort. Making the most of it, he said, "It sure will, Ben. I look forward to that day when Bethy and I start our own family." He gave Beth a slow grin as she brought her head up and looked at him directly, with pure dislike. "I know she does, too."

Beth pushed her chair back from the table, hurriedly. "Excuse me... I—I'm not feeling well—"

Jimmy rose quickly, noticing Bobby's arrested movement as he started to rise and come to Beth's aid.

"Beth—" Ben said. But she'd already started to run for the kitchen door. Ben looked helplessly at Jimmy.

"Maybe the food isn't sitting well with her." Jimmy shrugged.

"Or the conversation," Bobby observed, taking another bite of his food, apparently unworried.

Jimmy whirled on him, unable to contain his anger. Why did Bobby have to come here and ruin everything? *Everything!*

"This doesn't concern you," Jimmy said tightly.

"Jim!" Ben warned.

Jimmy turned to face the older man, trying desperately to gain control of his emotions. He felt his life, his dream, slipping away from him at breakneck speed. It was all crumbling, and now this sorry old man was calling him down in front of an Indian?

"I'm gonna go see about Beth." Jimmy gave both of the other men a defiant glare, daring either of them to stop him. Bobby returned the look for a split second before he masked it. Ben only gave Jimmy a long stare of disappointment.

As Jimmy stalked away, he heard Ben apologizing for him. "Jim's had a long day. He really didn't mean to be rude. I'm sorry for his bad behavior."

Bobby replied, "He's probably just worried about his fiancée, don't you imagine, Mister Halston?"

Jimmy angrily blew through the kitchen door. *It's come to this, the old man apologizing for me to the man who is ruining his daughter right under his nose.*

His mind shifted to Beth. Beth, who was nowhere to be found. He would not walk around calling for her like a lovesick fool! He took a few steps toward the woods, and even though the moon was bright, there was no sign of Beth.

There were a thousand places to hide. Having been raised here, Beth could easily find each and every one. She could disappear for as long as she wanted. But, from the way she'd acted inside, she really had been unwell. Jimmy turned away from the looming darkness of the trees. If she were out there, being sick, she wouldn't appreciate a witness.

If she wasn't back inside in an hour, he'd go searching—even if it did make him look weak and worried.

He wandered aimlessly, loathing the idea of going back inside without Beth.

The river whispered to him, the soft murmuring and gurgling

of the moving water calling to him soothingly after the turmoil this "special day," as Beth had called it, had brought.

He wandered toward the river, his thoughts rolling over themselves as the lapping water seemed to do.

Beth had meant everything to him for so long. How long had she been cheating on him with Bobby? How long? His breath came in short bursts as he fought for control, his emotions raw and ragged.

A sound caught Jimmy's ear—the hitch of a sob, coming from a distance ahead of him. He started forward but didn't call out. He'd just follow the sound. Beth was not easily given to tears, which Jimmy admired greatly, but she did have her times.

Jimmy had always thought that theirs had been a match made in heaven, as so many others had said. Now, it was hard to imagine a life without her. When Beth gazed up into Bobby's face this afternoon, Jimmy had known he'd lost her forever. There was going to be no reconciliation. By that look, Jimmy had realized Beth was more in love with Bobby than she'd ever been with him.

But what could come of it? Ben was one of the most prejudiced men Jimmy knew—in Cochise County or anywhere else, for that matter. Though he put on a façade of being fair and treating all men equally, Jimmy knew that was not truly the way Ben thought.

Often enough through the years, Jimmy had watched Ben. He'd tried to emulate him, knowing one day the Circle H would be his. Ben had done *something* right, building a ranching empire almost single handedly. He'd been here in the old days, when the Apache had been a real, true threat to everyone who'd dared to settle in this part of the Arizona Territory. He'd carved a home for himself and his family in this wild country—and that strength was something Jimmy envied.

Ben's weak spot was the same as Jimmy's—Beth. After Beth's mother had died, the hard-bitten rancher softened toward the little girl he'd barely given notice to during the first three years of her existence. He included Beth in everything he could think of, teaching her to ride, shoot, rope—everything he would have taught a son, if he'd had one.

Alberta had been in charge of the household, just as she'd been before Lenore had died, and things continued in a steady vein through the years. From Alberta, Beth had learned to be a lady. And to never look down on anyone...even the Indians.

Another sob sounded, pulling Jimmy out of his thoughts. He stopped to listen.

"Beth—"

"Oh, Bobby—"

In a small clearing several yards away, Beth rushed into the open as Bobby also came into view from the opposite direction, leading his mount.

Bobby stopped and dropped the horse's reins as Beth rushed into his arms, turning her face upward expectantly. Bobby's lips crushed hers.

The passion in that kiss broke Jimmy's heart all over again.

Witnessing the raw need between Bobby and Beth now made Jimmy realize the lack of feeling between Beth and himself. He'd never known what he was incapable of until this very moment, seeing the two of them together like this. Up until now, he'd kept trying to convince himself that none of what he'd witnessed today was true.

Now, there was no doubt. He was not the one for Beth. All he felt now was sadness, and mounting anger. She'd led him on for—for who knew how long? Carrying on with another man right under his nose—and one who could never give her the things Jimmy could when he took over the Circle H.

Jimmy had plans for this place! Improvements that Ben would

never have thought of, or even agreed to, if someone else brought him the ideas and the know-how on a silver platter. *Stubborn old fool.*

Jimmy had never stopped to wonder one time what he'd do if he didn't marry Beth—it had always been such a certain thing.

Now, here was Bobby, kissing Beth right in front of him for the second time that day...stealing her all over again—

Jimmy's hand moved for his gun. The butt of the revolver was familiar and brought him some odd comfort despite what he was about to do.

Such a terrible thing... but this "special day" had brought nothing but terrible things. This was a fitting end to all of it. Let it happen all at once so it could be over. Finished.

He would kill her. He loved her that much. His first love had been Beth. He'd never wavered, all these years. But love also meant wanting what was best for her, didn't it?

His fingers tightened around the smooth grip of the pistol as he drew it from his holster. He brought it up swiftly and took aim at Beth's head. His finger pulled back slightly on the trigger.

How would he deal with this—this death of a dream? His knees shook, not from fear but from the whole enormity of what he was about to set in motion by the simple act of pulling the trigger.

He'd taken a life before, this would not be the first time. He was oddly grateful for having had some experience in this—the bringing of death to another.

"You better holster that pistol, James Richard Franklin," a voice hissed from behind him. The unmistakable sound of a round being jacked into the waiting chamber of a Remington repeater sounded like thunder. He jumped and stiffened, his finger loosening from the trigger immediately.

"Turn around, Jimmy."

"Alberta, I—"

A shot rang out in the stillness of the July evening.

Jimmy's head jerked to look toward his left where the whine of the bullet had come from.

Beth gave a sharp gasp and began to slip from Bobby's arms. He held on to her and lowered her slowly to the ground, his gaze never leaving her, as if he were willing life into her, and didn't care if a second shot followed to claim him, as well.

Ben tipped the rifle downward, shoulders slumping, his eyes vacant.

"Ben!" Alberta screamed.

From behind him, Jimmy heard the heavy-set woman step forward. "Oh, my baby girl!" Alberta hurried past Jimmy toward where Beth lay in the clearing, Bobby kneeling beside her.

Jimmy's gaze held Ben's in the early darkness. Ben came toward Jimmy, shuffling wearily, as if there were no strength left in him. He'd aged a hundred years in the space of one afternoon.

Had Ben seen Jimmy aiming his pistol at the couple? At Beth? Had the older man been trying to kill Bobby rather than his own daughter?

Jimmy turned his attention back to the clearing. Beth—*was she dead?* He should go to her—

Alberta knelt beside Beth on one side, Bobby on the other. Jimmy would just be in the way. Paralyzed by what he'd almost done, he stood and looked at the scene unfolding.

"You fool men, get over here! We need to get her back to the house!" Alberta shouted.

"You wanted to kill her for love... for jealousy." Ben had come abreast of Jimmy, not looking at him. "I wanted to kill her for pride. If she had none, I had to let her know a Halston doesn't... doesn't have intimate times with an Indian. She needed to know that, Jimmy. She had to be taught."

At Jimmy's incredulous stare, Ben went on. "Yes, I've known about her and Bob for a long time. I gave her plenty of time to break it off with him, but—"

"You tried to kill her because she loved Bobby?"

Ben looked up at Jimmy with disbelieving eyes. "Well, now... didn't you do the same?"

Alberta's weeping could be heard in the distance, but everything else was silent in that summer twilight. Time stood still.

Ben stared accusingly at Jimmy. "Didn't you do the same, Jim?" After a moment, he shook his head. "Different ideas of why, but it was for the same reason."

"God help me...." Jimmy muttered. "But you're her father."

"Yes. And I loved her enough to stop her from making a mistake with her future. With him."

Jimmy's eyes filled with tears for the second time that day. "Why didn't you kill Bobby, Ben? Why?"

Ben shook his head with contempt. "And bring down the Apache on us, after all these years of peace? I'd not do that for anyone."

Ben turned away and walked toward the woods. He stopped and looked back at Jimmy one last time. "Maybe you weren't the man to take over this spread after all," he said quietly. "You'll have to live with what you almost did. Your thoughts... your anger... now, your loss."

He looked down, studying the ground, then turned toward the woods and once more started toward the dense blackness before him. "And God help me, so will I."

—Cheryl was born in Duncan, Oklahoma, and grew up in Seminole, Oklahoma, both small towns. Reading and writing her own stories were her fa-

vorite pastimes as far back as elementary school, which led to earning a B.A. in English from the University of Oklahoma. Writing westerns and western romance is in her blood, having been born and raised in Oklahoma, the product of at least five generations of proud Oklahomans who lived there when it was still Indian Territory.

She has also served as the President of the Western Fictioneers, a professional organization for western authors. In the past, three of her stories have been nominated in the Best Western Short Fiction category of the Western Fictioneers Peacemaker Awards.

Cheryl and her husband have lived in the Oklahoma City area for the past 40 years. She has two grown children and two fur babies.

GOLD RUSHED

CL STEELE

1849, APRIL 10, GOLD JOURNAL

Come pan for gold with me. The work is awful, but the money is plenty, and together, we'll never have to work another day," his letter had said. Gold desire rushed through my veins when I got my brother's letter. I told my wife I'd have to leave straight away. Time was a'wasting, and money waits on no man. She'd have cowhands to help her. I gathered up everything I needed for the month's travel. I kissed her and her pregnant belly, promising I'd send a letter as soon as I got to my brother's stake. She said she'd send a letter by U.S. Mail Packet and let me know if it was a boy or a girl. I assured her I'd be in California panning our gold future by June.

PS: That was the last day I remember being happy. 1849 April 10.

1849, MAY 4, GOLD JOURNAL

A thousand miles at thirty miles a day by horse on my own. Sur-
ly, I'd make it by June, allowing for rest and this dang drenching
weather. I could've joined a wagon train headed that way, but there's
trouble in numbers. I prefer doing it on my own. My decisions, my
fate, and all mine—the gold I'd find. I had my horse, Copper, and
hers, Lucky, carrying the pack. My dog, Rusty, insisted on coming
with me. A dog's love you can't buy. They require nothing from
you. I can guarantee that this dog will be with me all my life. In my
dreams, I could feel the pure nuggets of gold my brother told of in
his letter. I needed that security for my family. Cattle were fine, but
gold, now that was the rich man's life.

I must admit, though, I've wondered daily if my wife was still
thick with a child. Suppose I may already have a son or a sweet girl.

PS: The hardest thing about being alone is missing them. That
and this damn rain, that comes at sunset.

1849, May 15, Gold Journal

The last two weeks on this gold journey have been pure misery. I
know misery is the exception, and happiness is the rule. Gotta have
a bit of both, but between the missing and the rain, this pain seems
an omen. I won't let it stop me. Shoot, no, I'm stronger than pain.
But... today isn't the happy rule.

Rusty, my dog, who wouldn't leave me, well, today, that loyalty
proved fatal for my dear friend. In the middle of the night, when

the stars were bright, and the moon was full and high overhead, I fell asleep. Rusty woke me with vicious barking and snarling. I spotted the red glaring eyes of two or three of them and pulled my side shooter. My shots did little but scare the wolves off, too late for Rusty. One of them had attacked him, the neck bites too deep, though I tried to slow the flow of the blood from his jugular vein. I lay with him, holding my bandana on the wound, both of us looking only at each other. We both knew. Rusty whimpered. My eyes ached. I pulled him close so he couldn't see my pain, and after a few torturously long moments, my best friend put his head on my shoulder and went limp. I prayed for God to bring those tortuous moments back.

I spent a half day in the rain, lifting heavy mud by hand until the grave was deep enough. I buried my faithful friend in that blasted cold wind and rain. Drops fell on him from the rim of my stiff hat as I closed the grave and cursed the wolves. I looked for Lucky. But didn't have any luck. The shots had caused Lucky, my wife's horse, to rear that night, and while I grieved, she'd run off. I couldn't wait anymore—rain or pain or Lucky or not. I'd have to start tomorrow to make it by June. My family was counting on me. The gold called, and I had responsibilities. Sometimes, that's the thing that gets you through. I'll start out on the Carson Trail. I'll have to load up Copper and pare things down to the essentials. I wondered why I decided to come alone. Damn, stubborn, I suppose. Still, a man must do things his way.

PS: I left a large rock on Rusty's grave marked with his name. We'll find him and bring him home someday.

1849 Gold Journal, late May, Best I Can Figure

I've lost track of the days. Sleep's rare. The wilderness here is not kind to me, being alone. Still, there have been good times. The rain stopped for nearly a week now, and I shot the best-tasting rabbit. I found this meadow and watched for a day as Copper ate and ate and even reared and ran free in the sun for a bit. It did both our spirits good. The weather was definitely warmer, and the supplies were less for Copper's back. I used the trees for shade—my hat had blown away. But soon, I'd have a whole closet for nothing but hats. I think today I'm a dad—just a feeling. Son, I'm betting.

This morning, I packed up, and we headed out at dawn. I might get the last thirty miles done today if I was right. Even with the wrong turn, this military map and my marks seem to show me close to the gap that will lead to the town. The mountains are much taller now. Copper took careful steps through the gap at the end of the day. The rain was light, so I decided we'd head on until we got through the gap. Worst decision ever. Near dusk, Copper slid off a rock, spooked, and reared. I fell on the rocks and hit my head hard. My hand grabbed my skull, and with the red palm, I knew I might live, but the headache would remind me to think better next time. Then I saw my horse try to stand. My horse came up lame. I unpacked and unsaddled him, wrapping his fetlock with strands from my other shirt.

A day later, his breathing pained me as much as the pain hurt him. Staring into his trusting eyes, I hugged him, assuring him everything would be fine. I pulled away, pulled the trigger, and shot him through the back of his brain. He fell, never knowing what was coming. Lucky for him, not me. I will never get that memory from my head. It had to be done, of course. I carried what I could, leaving most of it along the Sierra Nevada Mountains and Carson Trail.

I was shunned by a group of wagons passing by. Nobody wants a stranger in their circle of wagons. They did say Sutter's Mill was two day's ride away. Just stay on the trail. Without much food or water and temperatures getting hotter, I must've made a few wrong turns out here. Sutter's Mill should've been just over this ridge, but it wasn't. Instead, I came across what cowboys like me call heaven.

It is the biggest lake I'd ever seen. It was clear, with fish practically jumping in my shirt as I ran it like a sail in the deep still waters. The scent of the pines surrounding the lake gave me peace, shelter, and some pine nuts to eat. Mountains from afar now provided beauty and protection from the cold, wet weather I'd walked through. I made a fire that night, ate fish after fish like it was my last meal, and stared at the glimmers of moonlight on the lake rippled by the soft, warm breeze. I spied on the natives, and they spied on me. I needed to get by this lake and to my brother. Just a day or two's walk to the other side, where the gold rushed through my thoughts of being enough to give me everything I'd need. That thought shut out the lapping of the lake as I leaned against the rough bark of the pine. Suddenly, I wondered if the gold would give me anything I'd already given up. The birth of my son, the eyes of my wife before her eyes begged me not to leave her, the dog that saved me, the horse that carried me. How much was I willing to let go of to reach a brother and gold and life I couldn't even imagine right now? Would it be easier without all I've already given up? Still, I thought. I've decided. I'm closer to the dream than I am to the home I left. What choice do I have but to carry on?

I stood and stretched. In awe of this place, I let my senses down a bit. The sun was rising fast. In the mid-morning sky, eagles flew overhead, diving at one another in a sky so blue it made the lake green with envy. This moment gave me the peace I sorely needed.

My day would end with my brother handing me a nugget of gold. I could feel it, feel the hope again.

It was silent. I felt the blood trickle down my back first, and the arrow poked its way through my right ribs. When I felt the heat and pain, I fell to my knees. I couldn't call out. I couldn't breathe. Things went from sky blue to black.

Next, I knew, these natives were hauling me into a small grass house made of sticks and woven tall grass. Their women tried to heal me. They called themselves the Washoe. Didn't like the gold rush crowd encroaching on nearby lands. Best I could figure, they'd lived here since the beginning and called the lake Tahoe or Dawoe as best as my ears could hear it.

1849, At Least Mid-June

I escaped under the new moon. I left Lake Tahoe, working my way toward California. I had taken some of their food and these blue-gray rocks that contained silver. I could only walk ten or so miles a day. Each day in the heat, I've grown weaker and sicker. The wound was red and smelled of pus, the ribs hurt with every step, and the breathing wasn't easy. But what choice did I have but to walk to my brother and that thought of gold that used to rush my blood? Now, all I wanted to know was if my wife was okay, if the ranch was good, and if I had a son. I suppose my brother was still mining gold or maybe looking for me.

1849, Likely Still June, Maybe Later, Gold Journal

No one would know now if I lived or died or how rich I was or wasn't. I'd be no more than meat for the wolves and dirt for the worms. With this blue-gray rock beside me, I wrote my final words in this journal, the only thing left to me.

I'm sorry, my Sara, and if my brother finds me the rock is silver, the map shows you where to find it when the Gold is out. I've no regrets, I wrote. Thought he'd believe that. I did what I thought was best. I lived on the land that gave me strength and soothed my soul, and though I didn't get my gold dream, I fought for it, and that is all any animal or human can do. Surviving as long as we can toward what we know we want—feeling the dream and living the freedom would be the lesson of my life. But in my heart, I knew the lesson was that love was more than gold could ever bring. I put the leather journal under my shirt near my heart and held the stone in my hand. I closed my eyes some time amid dawn, resigned to meet a new heaven.

Signed, Ethan Grosh

PS: If this journal is found, see the map to my home and wife Sara and my brother Hosea mining in Sutter's Mill, because some things are purer than gold nuggets.

Years Later Covering the time period of 1854-1864

The gold rush ended partly because I found this dead man and his journal. He seemed to have had a rough go and never reached the gold. However, the silver in his hand started the silver rush on the other side of the Sierra Mountains near the Carson Trail. He will never know how he changed the world. I used his maps and, in 1859, found a vein of silver so big it kicked the gold rush to silver. After the silver mine got dug, and I'd gotten more than enough, I returned his journal to his widow, and we sent a letter to his brother. Soon after, we married. Today, his son turns fifteen. He calls me Dad. It's time he gets to know his real dad, too. I'm giving him his dad's journal and his share of the silver mine for his birthday. He has a girl he wants to marry. I hope he reads this last entry and knows the sacrifices, both his dads, made for him. The dreams we made come true both out of fortune and misfortune. Without one, we'd not have the other. The difference is knowing that misfortune makes us stronger and fortune makes us braver, and both take life and make life. Life is a wild ride where the best we can hope for is that the good days outweigh the bad.

PS: Live YOUR life. MAKE your peace.

Signed,
Henry Tompkins Comstock—your second dad.

—CL Steele has been writing for eight years with many published works in the short story field. While she writes poetry and romance, she also writes science fiction, horror, and Westerns. The story for her is the relationship of the characters and the connection they make to the here and now, regardless of the setting being a deep space, a quaint cafe, or the Wild West. If you like stories with a twist and a punch, you will enjoy the writings by CL Steele.

A JACKTAW BANK ROBBERY

BIG JIM WILLIAMS

BUDD SUGGS LOVED his coffee. He wanted it scalding hot, thicker than molasses or road tar, and strong enough to float a pregnant Clydesdale horse.

Budd was a character. At least, most said so.

"Had a long nose and matching feet you'd see coming around a building before you'd see him," claimed his bunkhouse buddy, "Moon" Merkle, who was closer to Budd than tight shorts.

Morning coffee got Budd's eyes open, mouth moving, heart ticking, and blood flowing. He put more grounds in the pot than water and let it boil and thicken up for a couple of days before biting some off, or tongue-slurping it up from a cup, saucer, or swallowing it right from the bubbling pot's dripping spout. Since one cup could wake the dead, Budd kept it away from funeral homes and graveyards, unless trying to revive someone who owed him money.

Budd was a saddle-riding cowboy since his floor crawling, thumb sucking days. He climbed onto his first horse—weren't no hobby-horse—before he was milk weaned. Held the reins high and booted a gelding into a faster departure than a woman's lover window-exiting when hearing her husband enter the front door.

As a young man, Budd served as a U.S. Marshal in Abilene and Dodge City, Kansas, Tombstone, Arizona, and other wild cow-crossings that needed taming. He used his six shooters and fists. A pistol whipping, or punch in an Adam's apple brought most lawbreakers to their knees faster than a bridegroom begging for sex.

Budd was now older and down on his luck, having trouble scrounging free drinks at the Bent Rail Saloon in Jacktaw, a remote Texas crossroads with more cow pies, flies, fleas, and stray dogs, than people. Budd was an aging wrangler in a town of three saloons, one hotel, a barbershop, a gunsmith, restaurant, numerous upwind privies, and Madam Green's Saloon & Pleasure Palace north of town.

Jacktaw was named after General J. Hickenlooper Jacktaw, who defeated superior Yankee forces at the famous Battle of Goose Creek in the U.S. and Confederates' un-Civil War of 1861-65. When the general died, they planted him near Ma Green's Saloon & Pleasure Palace so he wouldn't be lonely. His tall, obelisk historic grave marker states:

GENERAL J. HICKENLOOPER JACKTAW
1823-1868
CONFEDERATE WAR HERO.
DEFATED 1,000 DAMNED YANKEES IN
THE HISTORIC BATTLE OF GOOSE CREEK, GEORGIA,
JULY 4, 1863.
GONE, BUT NOT FORGOTTEN.
RIP

They wanted to bury the general riding his one-eyed horse, Cyclops, but the gravediggers went on strike that week, so former Texas' men-in-gray soldiers dug the deep, accommodating hole. The funeral's big turnout included Madam Green's Shady Ladies—including Mae Belle Potts, the general's favorite—plus the defeated Goose Creek Yankee officer who praised and saluted the general for his victory. The two-hour eulogy, written by the general, included reenactment scenes from the battle. It was read by teary-eyed, whiskey-voiced Madam Green, who ended the sad farewell by offering free beer, pickled eggs, and senior discounts in her house of pleasure. As funerals go, the Jacktaw Clarion newspaper called it, "A danged fine sendoff."

Budd Suggs drank the beer and chewed some pickled eggs, hiccupped all night, and would have taken advantage of Madam Green's bedroom discounts, but was broke, had bad credit, and thought Mae Belle's charms should also be free, something she refused. "But I love you, Mae Belle," he pleaded.

"Budd, honey," said the mattress actress, crossing her long legs and buttoning her bosom-busting blouse, "you ain't really loved anything since your daddy—one of my best customers—gave you a puppy when you were still crawling in diapers and sucking sugar-tits."

"That's not fair!"

"Exactly what your daddy said when I doubled my rates, and Madam Green closed early and stopped giving away pickled eggs."

———————◈◈◈◈◈◈◈———————

"IF MY POCKETS get any emptier," said Budd, "I won't need 'em. The only thing in 'em is lint and holes."

"So…," replied "Moon" Merkle, Budd's short sidekick whose bowed legs made wishbones envious. He was in his late thirties, had fat cheeks, a hairless head, a graying mustache, and looked as unhappy as a politician who missed last month's graft money.

"I need money, and it ain't growing on trees," explained Budd, whose tall, thin frame matched his needle nose.

"So...?" questioned Moon.

"Let's go get some."

"Any suggestions?"

"Sure."

"What?"

"Rob the Jacktaw Bank."

"Budd, you're crazy."

"It's where the money is."

"Yep, in a big vault."

"Let's do it."

"Just waltz in and say, 'Gimme all your cash money?'"

"A loaded pistol helps."

"Well, I don't know. The law frowns on robbing banks."

"So I heard."

"So, you really wanna rob the Jacktaw Bank?"

"Tomorrow's good. I ain't got nothing planned except an eighteen hour workday on the ranch, and a nap."

"You'll miss your afternoon nap if we rob the bank, cuz we're gonna be running out of town with a hundred angry depositors on our asses, cuz we're stealing their life savings. It won't make us popular."

"I've thought about that."

"Running... getting caught... or being popular?"

"We'll rob the bank at 10:30 Thursday morning. Then escape on the cattle train that leaves Jacktaw Thursdays at exactly ten forty-five."

"Tomorrow's Wednesday," clarified Moon.

"Then we'd better wait a day."

"And if that posse catches us, they'll hang us."

"I've also thought of that," said Budd.

"You have?"

"They can't hang us," smiled Budd, "cuz Jacktaw's surrounded by desert and ain't got no trees."

"But a posse shooting bank robbers dead works. Have you thought of that?"

"I'm thinking on it."

"I ain't sure I wanna rob the Jacktaw Bank," said Moon.

"But, there ain't no other place in town that's got money, unless it's a kid's piggy bank."

"That's an option," said Moon.

BUDD AND MOON tightened their gun belts, used their dirty bandanas as masks, squinted to try and look mean, and stepped into the bank on Thursday morning at exactly 10:30.

"Get 'em up," yelled Budd, waving his rusty, unloaded gun. "This is a hold up. Give us all your money."

The bank's manager, Mister "Bubba" Jones Calderon the Third, a fat man wearing an aging three-piece suit with more shine than a saloon mirror, smiled a cheery hello. "Ah, good morning Budd Suggs and Moon Merkle, always good to see you boys. I see you're out this morning doing a little play-acting like mean ol' outlaws Frank and Jesse James while pretending to rob our bank. Nice outfit you're wearing. Like your masks. You're always welcome in the Jacktaw Bank where our business slogan is, 'We Protect yer Money better than hiding it under yer mattress, or burying it in yer backyard.'"

Budd and Moon pointed their single-shot, black-powder pistols.

"Are you two here this morning to make a deposit or withdrawal?" questioned the lumpy banker.

"This is a real bank robbery!" shouted Budd. "Put all your money in this sack." He tossed a burlap bag onto the counter.

Mr. Bubba Jones Calderon the Third, laughed. "Be with your fellers as soon as I help Mrs. Bessie Ringwald. She's making a payment on her forty-acre ranch outside of town. Nice little place with running water, grazing cattle, and two outhouses near a corn crib."

"Good morning Budd and Moonie," said Mrs. Ringwald.

"Morning," said the two, tipping their hats.

"Nice seeing you boys, again," continued Mrs. Ringwald, adjusting her glasses, feathered hat, and bustle. "I agree with Mister Calderon that you two should be thinking about becoming play actors, traveling around the country putting on wild west shows like Buffalo Bill Cody and Ned Buntline. Why I remember seeing 'em in—"

"Nope, this is a real holdup," said Budd, doubling his squinting, really trying to look mean.

"Budd, that's good," smiled Mr. Calderon, "the way you delivered that line, play-acting like real show people. Yes, sir, real believable. Now, if you two will step aside, I'll take care of Missus Ringwald's business, and be with you showbusiness boys in a minute."

The dejected Budd and Moon reluctantly did.

The bank president, clerks, and customers gave the would-be-bank bandits cheers and a big round of applause.

"Budd, this ain't working out the way we planned it."

"They ain't taking us seriously," muttered Budd.

"Now, what'll we do?"

"Don't know, but I think we'd best leave."

They stepped outside, removed their masks, holstered their pistols, and plopped onto a bench reserved for bank customers.

"Dang-it, Moon, this has been a mighty big disappointment."

"No one believed us." Moon shook his head. "And I'm still broke with empty pockets. If I had two nickels to rub together, I'm sure I'd be wearing someone else's pants. We can't even convince people we're low-down evil bank robbers. Another potential career lost."

"Guess we'll go back to being cowpokes working long days in the snow or heat," sighed Budd, "branding cattle...."

"... eating dust...."

"... living with sore butts, stiff legs...."

"... and aching backs...."

"... in bug-infested bunkhouses, eating...."

"... tough steaks, greasy bacon...."

"... and biscuits with cold gravy...."

"... while downing hot, thick, strong coffee...."

"... and getting drunk Saturday nights with Mae Belle Potts in Madam Green's Saloon and Pleasure Palace."

"My sweet momma," said Moon, "warned me such days would be a-coming."

Budd went to whittling on a stick, while Moon began chewing tobacco and spitting.

"Now, hold it right there fellers," said a deep, stern voice.

"What...?"

It was town Marshal Karl Clapshaw. "There's a five dollar fine for whittling and spitting here in Jacktaw," said the man with a badge.

"There is?" questioned the failed bank robbers.

"Either pay the five dollar fines on each of you... or go to jail."

"But we're broke, Marshal," they pleaded, scattering lint, turning their pockets inside out.

That's how the two spent a night in the Jacktaw jail, where Budd Suggs complained, "Their danged coffee ain't no good. Ain't hot, thick enough, black enough, or strong enough. It's thinner than a politician's promises."

Once released, Budd said, "Maybe, cuz of my great play-acting experience in the bank, I may just give up eating dust and herding cattle, and get to New York City and become a cowboy-acting star on the Broadway stage. I hear you can earn over thirty dollars a month doing it, meet lots of good-looking women, drink cham-pag-nee out of their open-toed boots, and dance all night. Maybe I'll become famous and get my picture in the newspapers."

"That," said Moon, "is about as unlikely as finding free beer at a church revival, clean sheets in a brothel, or us owning a cattle ranch."

BUDD SUGGS AND Moon Merkle never performed their bank-robbing act on New York's Broadway stage, or again in the Jacktaw Bank, but their names, for high crimes and misdemeanors—whittling and spitting—are forever etched in Marshal Clapshaw's historic arrest records in Jacktaw, Texas.

Budd Suggs thinks there should be a monument to them like the one for General J. Hickenlooper Jacktaw. Moon Markle disagrees, but he's thinking on it.

—Big Jim Williams' latest short story appears in the anthology, Through Western Storms. *He's currently completing the Western novel,* A Man Called Cinch. *His novel,* A Desperate Cattle Drive, *won the Western Fictioneers' 2014 Peacemaker Award for Best First Novel. His other books include* Escape West, Border Justice, Texas Justice, Seeking Justice, Gallows Justice; Eye for an Eye; Jubal Beckman, Mountain Man; Tales of the Frontier, *and his short stories have appeared in several anthologies,*

including, Best of the West, Over Western Trails, *and* Under Western Stars. *He's a lifelong broadcaster, and humor and ghost story author.*

The Covered Wagon by W. H. D. Koerner

☙ FIDDLER OF FIDDLETOWN

BENJAMIN HENRY BAILEY

WHEN MY PARTNER and I arrived in the town, it did not have a name, which I found to be right peculiar. There was a small sign on the main street that looked like a good place for a name, but it was blank. What was on the sign though for those interested was the population which was holding at a small twelve citizens.

"Where the hell are we?" asked Bill Troot, my partner.

I looked around briefly and shrugged. "That sign don't have a name on it, and I do not see anyone nearby to ask," I said, tugging on the reins of my mule. "We can find out the name of this place once I take care of this thirst that is threatening to kill me. Looks to be a saloon up ahead."

When I said my thirst was trying to kill me, I damn well meant it. I had not had a drop of whiskey in a couple weeks, but it might as well have been a couple years. My gullet was starting to think that I had married a Bible thumper and was spending all my time in church.

Bill and I had been out looking for gold these last couple weeks, and the damned fool forgot to pack a jug or two of rye. When I found out we were bone dry, I could have shot him, and came near doing it too. Better judgment, however, intervened and I did not blow off Bill's head there in the California mountains.

We tied our mules to the hitching rail outside the tent saloon and glanced up at the crude sign hanging above the door, which was a flap. The sign read The Water Trough, which I imagined them actually having a water trough filled with liquor and it kind of excited me.

"Least they didn't forget to name their saloon," Bill said with a slight chuckle.

We walked in, and once our eyes adjusted to the light, we could see a couple of tables but there was no one seated. Behind a wood slab that was held up on wood barrels, stood a man washing some tin mugs.

"Howdy gents. What will you have?" the bartender asked.

I said, "I am hoping that you have a decent supply of whiskey that I can wash my innards with."

"You came to the right place because that is all that we have."

The man set us up with two mugs of whiskey and I told him to leave the bottle. After a thorough drowning of myself, I wiped my beard with the back of my dirty sleeve. The bartender's name was Harold and requested that we call him that.

"Say Harold, what the hell is the name of this town?" I asked.

"You gentlemen are just in time. We are thinking of having a town meeting tomorrow night to finally give the town a name."

I poured myself and Bill another drink. "Nobody thought to name this place when they started putting down stakes?" Bill asked.

"Lord knows we tried. The problem is that we have names suggested by different people and of course, those same people vote for their own so we do not get anywhere."

"Huh," Bill said with a quizzical look, "I'll be damned."

"But now with both of you here, maybe when we vote tomorrow night, we can actually have a winner."

I thought about it for a few minutes. We had been panning up and down the mountains and a little break in town sounded nice. "Harold, if you keep us stocked in the devil's juice, then you got yourself two votes."

THE TOWN WITH no name had very little to offer in the way of amenities but for two lonely mountain men, it served us just fine. We got a bath and a shave that left most of our facial hair intact, and after that we decided to see what this town had in the way of women. We were told that a small cabin had been built that housed the ladies of the night. Truth be told there was only one and she was not open for business as of yet. Putting aside that idea we decided to go back to The Water Trough.

This time in the saloon, there was another man present, sweeping up the rough, wood plank floor. He was an older gentleman, even older than Bill and I, and he was not walking very good. He was leaning more on the broom rather than using it to sweep.

The man tried to wave at us, but his right hand had a continuous shake to it. We waved back, and he smiled an almost toothless grin. He didn't say anything but went back to sweeping.

Harold walked in behind us. "I see you met Fiddle. He helps me keep up the place"

I leaned over on the bar. "How old is Mister Fiddle?"

"Mister Fiddle? No one really knows. He does not talk at all, and he has that constant shake. He came to town with another fellow a while back, but that poor bastard fell dead the day after they arrived.

He seemed to have Mister Fiddle in his charge so after he died, there was no one to take care of him."

I glanced back over my shoulder and Mr. Fiddle was waving at us again. I smiled and waved back. Turning back to Harold, "Why does he go by Fiddle?"

"We never got that story either. The best I have been able to tell, he just fiddles around. I pay him some for his time and let him sleep in a shack out back."

"That is mighty Christian of you," Bill said.

The whiskey was a good brand and Harold kept them coming to us. After a while, I decided that I wanted to quench my thirst of another kind. "Boys, if you would excuse me, I am going to go sin in a different way." Leaving them at the bar, I left the tent and inhaled the dusk air. This town was growing on me, and I was not one for towns usually.

THE DOOR OPENED after my knock and what I saw was an angel. Standing there like a damn fool, I couldn't tell you what I said. It hadn't been too long since I was last with a woman of the night, but the figure I saw standing there made my mouth stop working and my eyes grow big. She let out a little chuckle and took my hand, leading me into her place of work.

She told me that her name was Goldilocks. Now before you say anything, yes, it is just like the damned fairytale. Her hair was long and as gold as the rock we were spending our lives looking for. She took some of my gold dust and let me tell you, I felt like I had died and gone to heaven. Once we concluded our business, I felt more drunk from that experience than I did from the whiskey.

I pulled on my boots as she draped a shawl around herself. "You going to be at the town meeting tomorrow night?" Goldie asked me.

Still finding words hard to say, I mumbled, "I figured so. We heard there is an issue with coming up with a name for this place."

She let out a small giggle, "We do have some conflicting ideas for the name. I want to name it Sunshine Valley, but I am the only one who has voted for it."

"Maybe I will vote for that," I said, standing up. I put my hat on my head and turned toward the door. "Thank you for a great evening, Miss Goldie."

———————⟨⟩———————

BILL AND I set up our tent a little way from town. After the evening I had, sleep was no problem. Bill had decided that he wanted to have a turn with Goldie so he was gone and by the time he returned I was out for the night.

The next morning, we found another tent not far from The Water Trough that served breakfast. They had freshly laid eggs, bacon, biscuits, gravy, and coffee. I was willing to pay their prices and ordered five eggs. The cook was from Ireland, and that man could cook. Some people might not think that egg cooking is a talent, and usually on the trail you get what you got. But Liam O'Brien was an artist in cooking food.

Our bellies were full and a walk was in order, otherwise Bill and I were going to find ourselves asleep under the table. Near The Water Trough was a wagon that had brought newcomers to the town. Two men, with lumber and furniture in the back of the wagon were here to set up shop. They wanted to open a hardware business and were going to stop at the first town that made them feel at home.

That was a risky way to find a town in my opinion because most towns don't make you feel at home and take most of your money.

The town had grown to have four newcomers over the last day and now it seemed that there was a real good chance of a name being decided. The meeting was to be held at The Water Trough as they had the most tables. Goldie was at one of the tables with some other folks from town that Bill and I had not had the chance to meet yet. I saw the hardware boys holding a violin and bow trying to use it to get a drink as it seemed they were low on income. Harold reluctantly agreed but did say that he did not know what he was going to do with a fiddle as he didn't know how to play. Laying it across the bar, the violin bought the hardware boys two drinks each.

Out of the corner of my eye, I saw Mr. Fiddle staggering among the tables. He seemed focused on the two hardware boys. His right hand was shaking, and he was making a low grumbling noise. The two hardware boys turned and looked at him.

"Is he okay?" one of them asked.

Harold was watching Fiddle make his way toward the bar. "Mister Fiddle? You doing alright?"

Fiddle laid both hands on the bar and the grunting stopped. He very gracefully picked up the violin and bow. Holding the violin in his left hand, he brought it up to his shoulder. The bow shook in his right hand, but he was able to bring it up to the strings. The crowd in the saloon became quiet, all eyes on Fiddle.

The bow touched the strings and let out a slight screech as the shaking was making it difficult to hold it still. We all watched in anticipation, not really knowing what was going to happen. I felt a deep sorrow for this man, who had lost his companion and become stranded in this town. He was lucky to have Harold, but doing tasks in a saloon was not for an old man.

I guess, though, I didn't know what would be good for an older man to do at his age.

Mr. Fiddle took a deep breath in and pulled the bow across the strings. The sound was rough on the ears but very quickly changed to a sweet melody. The shaking in the right hand stopped completely and the notes carried over the room. It took me a moment to realize that the song that he was playing was Amazing Grace. I had heard it a couple times in church when I was a child with my ma and pa.

Mr. Fiddle was not only playing the instrument with precision, but he started to move in a fluid motion as if the melody was flowing through his body. The bow would pull down across the strings and Fiddle would bend the same direction as if he was dancing to the music he was playing.

Now my time out west had been filled with things that the good Lord would probably take issue with, or at least that is what the fire and brimstone preachers liked to tell me. I had not felt much in my soul in my adult life and had tried to fill it with whiskey and women, and to be sure, those were some damn good times. Gold was the other filler I tried to use as something to give my life meaning. That night however, listening to this old man play sweet music filled my heart. I felt like the Lord was standing next to me, and the honest truth, I do not think there was a dry eye in that entire saloon. Mr. Fiddle had brought the Lord to us through his playing.

Now you might think I sound crazy, and if I was hearing this tale I would probably join you in thinking that. There is not really a way that I can even explain what we all felt. It was a miracle just being able to witness this man play. After Amazing Grace he went through some other hymns like Give Me Jesus and A Mighty Fortress is Our God.

When Mr. Fiddle was finished, he stopped and set the violin and bow back on the bar. Not one of us moved as we watched him do this.

He turned back around to face all of us and gave a toothless smile and a wave, his right hand had begun shaking again.

We all erupted in applause and Mr. Fiddle's smile just got bigger. "Well, now we know why they call him Mister Fiddle," Bill said, smiling ear to ear.

———————◆———————

IT WAS AGREED that the night should be more of celebrating Mr. Fiddle than voting on a name for the town. The meeting was rescheduled to be at noon the following day. Bill and I woke up the next day, a little hungover but feeling more alive than we had in a long time. We again had breakfast at O'Brien's and made our way back over to The Water Trough.

We were about to walk in when Harold came around the corner of the tent. He had a concerned look on his face and told us to come with him. We followed him toward the shack that Mr. Fiddle was living in. We glanced in and saw Mr. Fiddle still lying in bed. His face looked as it probably always did when he was sleeping. It could even be said that he had a slight peaceful smile on his face. Watching his chest, I realized that he was not breathing. The old man had passed away sometime during the night.

———————◆———————

WHEN EVERYONE MET for the meeting in the saloon it was heavy with a somber mood. Mr. Fiddle had been in his own way a part of the town and with him no longer here it felt as if something was missing and made one reflect on life.

The meeting progressed and names for the town were spoken.

I was not much listening to what was being said but was thinking of Fiddle. I wished that I could have known him longer and at that moment I just wanted to give him the world. I felt sad for him, that he had ended up here without any family to take care of him. Looking around the room though, I could see that the people of this town were his family, and he had gone out in this world apparently doing what he loved. He played that violin like there was no tomorrow and in his case that was true. When we had found him that morning, that peaceful look had shown that he did not feel pain when the Lord took him home, and I found that reassuring.

"Any other names that should be considered?" asked Harold.

I do not know what came over me, but I stood and removed my hat. "I have not been here long in this town, but I feel that I have been able to get to know some of you real well." I do not know why, but I could not resist looking over at Goldie who smiled briefly and winked at me. I looked away and cleared my throat.

"I think what we have all experienced over the last day was nothing short of seeing the Lord at work. Giving Mister Fiddle one last ride on the violin to make such sweet music before taking him home to glory. Now I am no preacher man, but I think that we should commemorate what we saw last night. Something that will let Mister Fiddle live on forever besides a name on a tombstone. I would like to have the name Fiddletown considered."

There were some mumblings of conversation among the townsfolk of the town with no name, and I suddenly felt foolish. I sat back down in my chair and looked over at Bill. "I would vote for that," he said with a smile.

Harold stood and called for a vote. The names were each called and to my surprise no one was voting for the names they had suggested. When Harold called out Fiddletown, everyone's hands shot into the air. Not even needing to take a count of how many voted, Harold smiled and said, "It's official! The name is Fiddletown!"

Everyone cheered and applauded, and Bill clapped me on the back and damn near knocked me over. Handshakes and hugs were given, and you would think a major victory of some sort had taken place. Harold opened the bar, and we all had a second night of celebrating. For the life of Mr. Fiddle and the new name of the town.

———

TIME PASSES AS it always does and those who can speak about what something is named for are no longer here to do so. There is an actual town in California called Fiddletown. It sprung up in 1849 with the gold rush but there is debate as to how the town came to have its name as there is no documentation. This story is purely fiction but a creative attempt to show how that town "might" have gotten the name.

———

—*A native to Colorado, Ben Bailey spends most of his vacations looking for new historical sites to visit through the American West. He fell in love with westerns at a very young age and in high school, he got an opportunity to be the first Gunfighter for a Day at Buckskin Joe in Canon City, Colorado. He was killed in each gunfight but luckily the crowd clapped and brought him back to life again. Ben desires to tell stories about the brave men and women from all walks of life that called the west their home.*

SAVE THE CHILDREN

BARBARA L. CLOUSE

INTRODUCTION

DISASTER IN THE California Territory during the Gold Rush meant thousands of deaths of the indigenous people living there. Some were killed by disease, but many others were murdered in cold blood.

———❦———

GREETING

"I AM NIKA Blue Feather, originally from the plains of Indian Territory. Our tribes were forced from eastern ancestral lands by the 'yellow devil' called gold. We continued to be banished by the presence of shiny stones in the Creator's Earth."

A group sat in the old chairs located in the abandoned church. The young woman stood near the wooden altar. Only a few candles were lighting the dark and burlap sacks covered the broken windows.

Nika raised her hand to get the attention of the women.

"You know who I am, sisters." She looked at each person. "However, by California law, I am known as Nettie St. Claire. I stood on the auction block at ten years old. A kind, Christian family bought me for a few coins. Your children were either killed in front of your eyes, or treated like slaves and shipped up north, or sent to the mines to dig for the gold's tracks and traces in the hard ground."

"Shall we pray," said a tall man on the front pew.

"Thank you, Pastor," offered Nika. "This ancient adobe structure has been a place of refuge and prayers, in the old days, when the Spanish came to conquer our farms and lands for the flag of Spain. The priests came next and other missionaries who read their Holy Bibles to us. Now the 'yellow devil' comes to scatter our tribes, ruin our rivers and forests, and has started the slaughter of our people.

"Brothers and sisters, we have endured enough pain. The day the soldiers came, I remember being sleepy and cold when the sun went down. Mother told me to 'hide like Moses.'

"I started reading the Bible at five years old. We lived and worked in the church near the Pine Lake Community. Mother and I practiced hiding at the water's edge, in the thick reeds of the shoreline. She told me bad men were coming and we had to save the children from our tribe.

"I had been to school, read the Bible, and understood the horror around us at ten years old. Mother always told me the truth, taught me skills a child should never have to learn, but her lessons filled me with courage and wisdom.

"Friends, you know my history, my family, and my tribe, who were all killed. That was the time I hid in the reeds while the soldiers attacked our village."

"'Hide like Moses' she said. I am so thankful my mother taught me how to survive."

"Brothers and Sisters of the Creator, if we cannot save the wisdom of our elders and the future of our children, we have nothing left of our people. Working together, we must protect the blood of our tribes."

MAPMAKER

THE CROWD QUICKLY disbursed and disappeared into the darkness of the night.

Nika noticed a stranger in the shadows of the church. She grabbed her long coat, blew out the candles, and hurried back to the newspaper office on the main street of the small town.

Nika was on a mission of survival. She needed a herd of mules and horses, plus several wagons full of supplies, to accompany her rescue plans. Now, she needed to find out who that dark shadow was hiding at the back door of the church sanctuary.

The lights were still on in the newspaper office, so she rushed to the weather-worn porch and its lantern of light.

"Reuben, you still here?" Nika called.

She heard grumbling from the back room, where the printing press and supplies were kept.

"Reuben, I've got one more article to do for tomorrow's edition."

"You won't have any newspaper at all, if I can't get this machine working. Sorry piece of broken trash!"

"Okay, I'll read the manual, and we'll work together."

A knock at the door surprised the young woman.

She opened the wide entrance and a tall man in leather and deer hides remained on the porch. "Can we help you, Sir?"

The man looked surprised as well and slowly stepped inside. "Pardon for such a late call, Ma'am."

"Please come in, Sir. Do we have any fresh coffee, Rueben?"

The white-haired old man went to the back room then returned with two mugs. "Here you go, princess."

Nika smiled. "Thank you, Reuben."

Nika offered one of the cups to the stranger and sat at her desk. She motioned for him to sit in the other chair and retrieved her writing tablet.

"Do you need something printed in tomorrow's paper or just get some posters made?"

"No, ma'am," he answered. "I have a letter for you from an old friend." He took a step closer and handed the package to Nika.

"Thank you," she said. "Would you like to have a sandwich with that coffee?" She pointed to the back room. The man nodded and joined Reuben. Nika could not imagine who her 'old friend' could be. Moments of the scenes in her childhood flashed by in an unfinished puzzle of colors and light. She closed her eyes and drifted back over the years, when she was in Indian Territory, far to the east.

Metal sounds echoed from the press room. The old printing equipment clacked and clanged. Reuben hollered from the back of the building.

"Hallelujah," he yelled. "He fixed the old heap of bolts and wheels!"

The young woman stood up and ran to the printer. "You fixed it!"

"Wasn't me," said Reuben. "Our guest pounded this old rattletrap back to life."

"Thank you, Sir. We appreciate your help." Nika shook his hand.

The long-haired stranger's hand was brown, but his eyes were bright blue. She finally looked at the mountain man-trapper's appearance and he seemed so familiar.

He smiled. "Been a long time."

The sound of his voice brought a flood of memories. Nika moved around the printing press and grabbed him in an embracing hug. "Antonio Estrada," she whispered. "We thought you were dead."

The young man removed his furry hat, his dirty deer skin coat and threw them in a pile in the corner of the room. "Nika Blue Feather," he smiled. "We thought you were taken up north."

She hugged him again. "I didn't recognize you under all that hair." She yanked on his beard and smiled again.

The two friends talked into the night, until dawn peeked through the front window of the newspaper's office.

"What happened to you, Tony?" asked Nika.

"I've been in hiding... lived up in the mountains for years, learning about trapping and hunting, and survival. After my people were all massacred at Stone Creek, I'd had enough, and I damned sure wasn't going to some priest school up north. I've seen our brothers who were caught and put in prison because they were Pawnee."

Tony looked at his dear friend. "Did you open your envelope yet?"

Nika grabbed the package on her desk. She unfolded the large paper. "What is this?"

"It's a map to the valley you've been dreaming about."

The young woman examined every inch of the weathered brown wrapping paper. "How did you do this?"

"I stayed with mountain men in the northwest, who taught me how to mark trails, and find my way to the rivers and valleys along the way."

"Tony, you've become a mapmaker!"

"Yes, I am, just because of you."

She grabbed him and they hugged the years away. Tears fell down her face as she thought about their childhood. Memories swept her back to those years of hiding and suffering losses, together on the plains of Indian Territory. The killing by the soldiers cost them their loved ones and their neighboring tribes, pushing everyone to an early death and the loss of the elders, even the children.

The small bands of teenage warriors worked together to protect the groups of grandmothers and grandfathers. Others helped the surviving young children to safe places in the western territories.

"Life is full of surprises, Nika." Tony offered. "I should have died several different times, but I ended up on a train to the northern religious schools."

"That was because you could read and quote some Bible verses," Nika reminded him.

"And—because I escaped that imprisonment, I grew up in the teaching ways of the Creator, and I survived."

"I'm so glad you did. You've brought me proof of the way to save the children."

Tony looked around at the newspaper office. "I was so worried about you. It looks like you were rescued as well."

"Yes, I stood on the porch outside and the church people gathered out front. There were about ten of us, both boys and girls. One by one, we were sold to the townspeople. I was very lucky to have been picked by the St. Claire family.

"Both husband and wife ran the newspaper business. Because they legally adopted me, I inherited this company when they died last year. Those gold mines brought all kinds of sickness and disease to our area. The tribes exposed to their madness died first and then the communities along the river, then to the farmers. We call it the 'plague of the yellow devil'—idiots from around the world have ruined our territory that's headed for statehood very soon."

"I may be a mountain man and mapmaker, but I need some grub."

"Well, I may only be a newspaper woman, but you also need a bath!" They both laughed as Nika turned out the lights and left the office. "Come stay at my place. I have a bathtub."

Ten years had passed by very quickly for the childhood friends. All those years ago, she had always wanted to travel with Antonio Estrada. She was sure about that. Nika cut his hair and he shaved most of his long beard off, while trimming his mustache. Tony soaked in the bathtub until Nika joined him. Their joyous reunion lasted all night.

Tony had dreamed about Nika for years. Traveling in the wilderness, learning about the map-maker skills helped his loneliness for home, for his family, and Nika Blue Feather. He thought of her every day, considering she might have died in all the violence occurring in the California Territory. He worried about the changes in her life and if she had been adopted by white settlers who took what they wanted from the tribal farmers and ranchers.

Now that he had seen her and felt her sweet caresses, he realized her spirit was the same—funny, caring, and a delight to fill the hours in the day. He looked forward to traveling to the hidden valley in the Idaho Territory with her.

"Hey, you going to sleep all day?"

Tony looked deep into the eyes of his best friend. "Why aren't you married?"

"Now that's a fine way to start the day!" Nika pulled the quilt over his face and tried to roll him out of the bed.

"You can't leave me now." Tony grabbed her and kissed her smiling face. They both rolled across the bed and slid to the floor.

"Get dressed," urged Nika. "We have plans to make."

THE PLAGUE WAGON

TONY AND NIKA walked across the yard to the barn built for her horses. They opened the huge door and closed it quickly behind them.

"I've kept this plan all to myself until old Reuben came out one day, unannounced. He needed to borrow some tools, and I just let him."

"These are the largest made wagons I've ever seen, Nika."

"I saw a picture of them in a newspaper ad from San Francisco. I didn't want anyone else from around here to get a look at them."

"If your wagons work with my ideas," added Tony, "we will be able to carry many people in these giant rigs."

Nika grabbed Tony and hugged him tight. "All we need to do now is paint the wagons with the 'plague' signs and we'll be ready to gather everyone."

After her adoption to the St. Claire family, Nika never had to work for the soldiers again. Just like the European plagues brought destruction to the most vulnerable in their midst, the smoke of death hovered over the villages and communities of the California Territory.

If she and Tony could finish the posters and signs, they would be ready to head north. The words stated— "smallpox" – "cholera" – "by order of the U.S. Army, this wagon is quarantined." The warnings of sickness and death would hopefully keep anyone from approaching the wagons loaded with the young and elderly passengers, plus food, supplies, and medical needs.

"Nika, it's so good to see you again," said the man in a new straw hat.

"Doctor Carlos Sandoval. I'm so glad you could come today," declared Nika. "We're ready for you to inspect our wagon train."

"If I know you, dear friend, you've got everything packed and ready to go."

"Yes, Sir. You are correct."

"Miss St. Claire, I do have a wish, for you to consider."

"What is that, Doctor Sandoval?"

"I would like to join your wagon train."

"By all means, Doc, I've wanted to invite you but was unsure you wanted to tackle such a long journey."

Dr. Sandoval took the young woman's hand. "Dear girl, I've known you since you survived that hellish attack on your village. I was assigned to that cavalry troop and hated every minute of the assignment. After their orders to annihilate the tribes, I retired from the Army. All these years, I've been hearing rumors about the valley of peace. Was that just a story or is there a real place?"

Nika smiled at the white-haired man. "Yes, there is, Doctor." She looked around the barn, then hurried to close the huge door. She pulled the folded paper from her apron pocket and laid it on a barrel lid nearby.

"One of my good friends from childhood arrived with this map. He escaped his train ride to the northern schools for boys when the soldiers were capturing everyone. He's been a hunter with mountain men in the northern territories, and learned about making maps, and marking trails along the way. He has been to the valley, and came here to find me, to help in our efforts to save the children and elders of our tribal family."

"That's good news, Nika. Since there will be older passengers, plus the small children, I'm assuming it would be helpful for me to tend your flock with medical care?" The doctor smiled and raised his medicinal bag for her to see.

Nika hugged the man then shook his hand. "Go pack your trunk of supplies, Doctor."

"Do you think it would be helpful if I wore my Army uniform, just in case we run into any soldiers on the way north?"

"Excellent point, Doc. We need to wear something to disguise who we are, as well. If our 'plague wagon' posters don't stop people, maybe if we wear bandanas over our noses, or put some marks on their arms, legs, and face?"

"Absolutely!" replied Dr. Sandoval. "That would help convince any nosy gold miners, lawmen, or the Army, that we're hauling patients of the plagues, and headed for the St. Francis Hospital in Oregon."

"Excellent ideas," added Tony. He walked over to Nika and kissed her cheek. "Getting closer to departure. Have you finished your business with the bank and your lawyer?"

"All done, Sir." Nika did a quick curtsey and salute for Tony.

"All the supplies have been deposited and packed on the wagons. Our drivers have arrived and disbursed to each farm," Tony explained.

"Sounds like we're heading north in the morning?" Nika smiled. "The elders and children will be moved from their assembly in the old adobe church to all the farms with our wagons."

"Yes, ma'am," answered Tony. "May the Creator be with us."

Nika shook her head. "Amen!"

GOODBYES

NIKA LOOKED AROUND her newspaper office. Even as a child, she remembered the talks around the campfire with her mother. She would group the smallest children together and share her thoughts in a story. Her tales were full of helpful animals, smart fish, and soaring eagles. Nika loved those magical times with the storyteller sharing faraway happiness. Now, after reviewing Tony's map, she knew that Peaceful Valley was real and not a myth.

Nika said goodbye to her friend Reuben, who was going to continue the weekly newspaper, with help from his two grown sons.

"I'll be back in one year, Reuben. I've talked to Mister Turpen from the bank and Mister Guthrie at the lawyer's office. They will monitor the funds from the paper business and the livery stable. Everyone will get paid, and if something comes up, please seek their advice. Mister and Missus Rodriguez will run the ranch for me, with the help of their sons."

"Safe travels, Miss Nika. We will surely miss you, ma'am."

"Thank you, Reuben. We'll be back soon."

WAGON TRAIN

SEVEN WAGONS, SEVEN grandfathers, seven grandmothers, seven children in each wagon. The mothers, who were recovering slowly from injuries, sent their infants to the wagon train. Dr. Sandoval shared with Nika that the women would not make it a week on the trail. Everyone hated to separate the mothers from their babies, but it was necessary. Two other nursing mothers, who had recently birthed their tiny babies, had enough milk to feed both children.

"Doctor, I am so pleased that we have an elder on each wagon. They were most hesitant at our meetings. The older children will be able to help with the younger ones. At our first stop, we must educate our "plague patients" as to what to do, if the soldiers follow us or try to delay our wagons."

"You are so right, young lady. All of us need to be prepared for such a confrontation."

At the midday stop near a small creek and shade trees, Tony assembled everyone. Biscuits with ham were served to the crowd, with canteens of water. Lunch was also served to the drivers, cooks, and scouts. Coffee was available to all since the slowness of the wagon train made everybody drowsy. A long trip needed plenty of stops to rest and rotate the horses, feed the children, and rest awhile.

Tony stood in front of the gathered adults, while all the children took naps in the shade. "Friends, we need to discuss our tactics. Doctor Sandoval will summarize his preparations for our wagon train."

"Most of you know that I was the medical staff for the Army assigned to Riverside. I also was available for the citizens of this community. After I witnessed the cruelty of the orders for the soldiers by our own President of these United States, I resigned my position. When I heard about the plans of these two young people, to not only rescue these precious children, but the adults and elders who wanted to leave as well, I was ready myself."

"When we discussed the ideas for disguising the wagons, adding 'QUARANTINED' was the most logical way to leave. I examined all the children and told the captain that they needed to leave the area, due to the most serious contagious malady that had crippled the young ones. I told the Army that the best way to protect the soldiers was to send the plagued children to the great hospital in Oregon."

The crowd clapped their hands and voices repeated "Praise the Lord" and "Amen brother!" Smiles and laughter filled the air as the group repacked the parked wagons to continue their day of travel.

As the weeks rolled by, everyone was thankful that no violent incidents had occurred. Both Nika and Tony knew about his scouts keeping a watchful eye on the perimeter of their route but said nothing to the travelers. Panic and worry would destroy the trust of the adults, in their effort to maintain a calm resolve for the children.

Tony pulled up beside Nika's wagon. She rode with the babies and helped the mothers in their dual duties of wetnurse for the youngest passengers.

"Everything all right?" asked Nika.

"My compadres from Rock Springs are approaching from the north. They are bringing news regarding the Territory of Wyoming. We need to keep up with any tribal wars going on. Word was passed to them that everyone was quiet at this time," explained Tony.

"Good to hear that. We don't want to roll into some incident this far away from anyone who could help us."

"I'll catch up with them and keep a low-profile. Be careful while I'm gone."

"Slow down and be careful yourself."

Tony spurred his horse and rode away to the east. The young man was not so worried about the tribes, but any dissatisfied soldiers could stir up troops in a heartbeat. He had been keeping an eye on Nika and already decided that he did not want to leave her again. After all the years they were apart, his love for her had grown. Marriage was the answer. Tony wanted her beside him every day and night forever.

The wagon kept up a slow, rocking pace, which was helpful for the babies in her care. Nika worried about her best friend trotting away from the group of armed drivers. She had longed for Tony for many years, and now that their lives had reconnected, she could not lose him again. She prayed for him, for protection from the evil ones in the rough country, and vicious killers who would shoot first and leave others to die.

The mountain men and trappers from the northwest gathered in the shelter of a small creek with cool water from the early snows of fall. They shared their findings of the tribes, and locations where the Army had camped throughout the area.

"*Senor* Estrada," called a huge man wrapped in multiple furs.

Tony hugged the giant man and offered him some cornbread freshly made that morning. "A present from Nika, old man."

Tears ran down the weathered face of the hunter. "You are almost to the valley, friend. We've been trailing you for a couple of weeks now. Winter comes right behind you."

"Thanks, that's what I wanted to know. Nika sends her love."

"You found the angel you talked about?"

"Yes, Goliath. I'm so thankful that I jumped off the train all those years ago."

"Me, too, little David. I've been thinking about that Bible you read to me on those cold winter nights when we were all snowed in from the storms. Do you think I'm too old to learn how to read?"

"No, sir. My Nika could teach you. Would you ride with us awhile, and she'll get started on that Bible?"

"Thank you, son. I never had any boys of my own. I'd be proud to accompany you, wherever you go."

"Goliath, that would be an honor, sir."

The two friends shook hands and hugged like father and son.

The group of trappers and mountain men slung their furs and salted meat on the back of their mules and horses and set off to join the wagon train. They arrived at noon the next day and joined the travelers for lunch. Forward scouts joined the growing crowd of wagon train drivers. Their fast pace alerted Nika and Tony's friends. They knew something was up.

"All the tribes are gathering," whispered Nika.

"What does that mean?" asked Tony.

"One of your forward scouts arrived last night. You saw the others who just arrived. They were frightened. These guys are not afraid of anything, but something has happened."

"Goliath?" asked Tony

The man shook his head. "I am puzzled as you are."

One of the elders stood with the children around their wagon. He nodded at Nika. She knew that he wanted to talk with her. He was the man who had pulled her from the water in the lake so long ago. He saved her life and Nika never forgot his kindness and bravery. The young woman weaved her way through the crowd to him.

She took his arm and they walked away from the adults and the children. "What disturbs the thoughts of a brave man?"

"The dreamers of my clan see feathers far away."

"Do they wear the paint of war, my dear friend?"

"No. Many feathers are in their hair."

Nika smiled and nodded her head in agreement. "That is good words from our dreamers."

Nika hurried back to Tony and grabbed his arm. "We must take a walk—*now,*" she whispered. "The dreamers say huge bands of people come quickly. It is not in haste. They are wearing the feathers of joy, not war."

"Nika, what does that mean?"

She smiled and kissed him. "The Elder says the group who will assemble with us is for support, not bloodshed. There is no warpaint on their faces or horses."

"Good grief, you remember all that stuff?"

"Yes, sir, I do. I'm a dreamer myself. I see the future when others do not."

PEACEFUL VALLEY

LEGENDS HAVE BEEN shared by the Tribes about a hidden valley in the northern territories that was full of life, plenty of water, a river, a lake, thick forests of pine, and enough game to feed many families. The most important characteristic was that this heavenly place was blessed with peace in a troubled country.

Nika stared at Tony's map spread out on the ground. They both read the trail they had just followed all those weeks ago. Hearing the prediction that winter would be starting soon, Nika wanted to make sure everything was timely since everyone was eager to find the end of the wagon trek and get settled in before the harsh weather of the Idaho Territory began.

Tony placed his hand on the map. "We're a few days from the front door of the valley, Nika."

"Oh, my," she whispered softly. "It's unbelievable that we made it here, with no injuries, no broken wheels, no violence. I am so thankful."

Tony grabbed her hand and held it in his. "The Creator was with us, kept us safe, and led us here, Nika."

"And—he helped us find each other again."

Their quiet moment together was interrupted by a scurry of activity at the beginning of the long line of travelers. Goliath stood in front of the first wagon and waved to the scouts and his hunting friends to assemble there. "Indians," he mumbled. "Savages approaching."

Tony retrieved his spyglass from his saddlebag and smiled.

"Nika Blue Feather, our tribes are coming."

He handed her his field telescope and nodded at the horizon to the east.

From north and south, east and west, groups of horses mounted by men in their tribal finery galloped closer. The feathered and beaded costumes were colors of the earth and sky, the green forests, the rising sun, and flaming fires. The regal representatives of each tribe carried a tribute flag for the children and elders in the wagons to see.

"Are they our escorts to the valley?" cried Nika. Warm tears rolled down her weary face.

He hugged her until her sobbing slowed.

"You did this, didn't you?"

Tony nodded as he watched Nika wave to the riders.

The horsemen trotted along with the wagons, while the children waved their handkerchiefs at them.

Tony could barely talk at the sight of their brothers surrounding the seven wagons. "My friends from the trapper, hunting, and map-maker days wanted to honor our rescue of the elders and children. They all knew exactly where the Peaceful Valley was located."

"What a surprising way to end our journey," whispered Nika.

"May the Creator continue to bless our days together," added Tony.

"What do you mean 'our days together'?" Nika asked.

Tony moved his horse closer to the wagon. He wiggled his fingers to catch her attention, then grabbed her and loaded her onto his lap. She giggled and held him tightly.

"Well, ma'am, I thought we'd get married first, here in the valley. Then, if you're up to it, we could head east and go rob a train or two."

"Look, robbing trains is against the law, Antonio Estrada. I don't want my name and photograph on the front cover of my own news-paper stating I was a train robber."

"Nika, slow down. It's not exactly stealing."

"How many kinds of robbery are there, Mister Lawyer?"

"We'll just be helping a bunch of boys get off the northbound train and head west. I thought you were still in the 'Save the Children' business!"

Nika Blue Feather was speechless. She opened her mouth to reply, but she could not speak a word. The young woman took a deep breath and looked at her best friend. "Did you say 'married'?"

———————————⊰◈⊱———————————

—*Barbara L. Clouse is a retired federal paralegal living on a farm in Musk-ogee, Oklahoma, with her husband, Jerry. Her children's book, The Healing Lodge, earned the prestigious Will Rogers Medallion Award Gold Medal in the Children's Illustrated category in 2023.*

When she's not helping with the family garden, Barbara enjoys teaching art, sewing, exploring genealogy, and researching her Cherokee heritage. A dedicated Sunday school teacher for many years, she has worked with children of all ages, sharing her passion for learning and creativity.

Hosting family gatherings and tackling fun projects with their grandchildren keeps the Clouse country home bustling and blessed.

In Old Wyoming by Frank Tenney Johnson

HAT CREEK

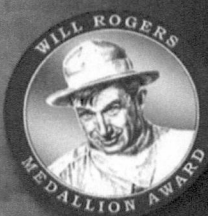

"A man only learns in two ways, one by
reading, and the other by association
with smarter people."
—Will Rogers

WILL ROGERS
MEDALLION

RECOGNIZING EXCELLENCE IN WESTERN MEDIA AND STORYTELLING AND COWBOY POETRY

www.willrogersmedallionaward.net

AN EPIC JOURNEY OF RESILIENCE, HONOR, AND THE RELENTLESS PURSUIT OF JUSTICE.

As the trusted lieutenant of the infamous Geronimo, Chato's days are painted in the hues of raid and revolt until personal tragedy strikes when his family are taken into slavery in Mexico. Hoping to secure their release, Chato strikes a deal to aid the U.S. Army in maintaining peace with his people. But when Geronimo denounces him as a traitor and departs, all hope for Chato's family flees with him. Forsaken by his former brothers-in-arms, Chato vows to hunt down the renegades himself, becoming a beacon of the Chiricahua peace faction clinging to reservation life in the process.

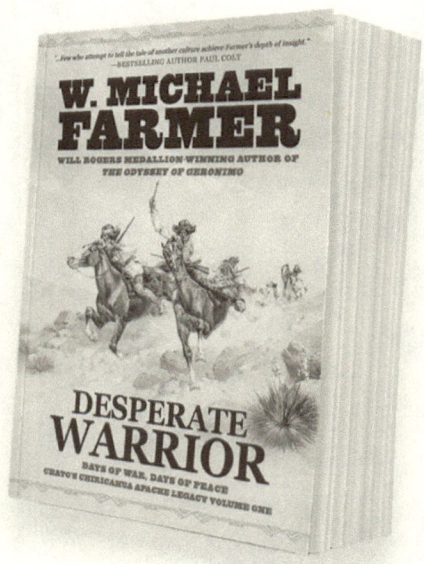

"... Few who attempt to tell the tale of another culture achieve Farmer's depth of insight."

—Bestselling Western author Paul Colt

Don't Miss W. Michael Farmer's other award-winning novels from Hat Creek, including The Odyssey of Geronimo: Twenty-Three Years a Prisoner of War *and* The Iliad of Geronimo: A Song of Blood and Fire. *Available at your favorite local bookseller*

The Perfect Combination.

Big Nose Kate Whiskey & *According to Kate:*
The Legendary Life of Big Nose Kate, Love of Doc Holliday